"Are you going to the birthday supper celebration tomorrow?" James asked.

Mari nodded. "Sure am."

"We'd be glad to have you and Zachary ride with us."

"Are you certain we'll all fit in your buggy?" she asked.

He grinned. "The more the merrier. Besides, if you come along, I won't have to drive with one of my sister's twins in my lap. You can hold him."

She laughed with him. "I'd be glad to come with you." And then she just stood there for a moment looking at him.

I think he's the best friend I've ever had, she thought. *Better than any man I've ever known. I trust him to do what he says he'll do. And he's been such a help with Zachary.*

"Good," James said. He met her gaze and then held it.

It was a strange moment, standing there, her looking at him, him looking at her. As if there was something else to be said, but she couldn't think what it could be.

"See you tomorrow, James," she finally said, making herself walk away.

"See you tomorrow, Mari."

Emma Miller lives quietly in her old farmhouse in rural Delaware. Fortunate enough to be born into a family of strong faith, she grew up on a dairy farm, surrounded by loving parents, siblings, grandparents, aunts, uncles and cousins. Emma was educated in local schools and once taught in an Amish schoolhouse. When she's not caring for her large family, reading and writing are her favorite pastimes.

Books by Emma Miller

Love Inspired

The Amish Matchmaker

A Match for Addy
A Husband for Mari

Lancaster Courtships

The Amish Bride

Hannah's Daughters

Courting Ruth
Miriam's Heart
Anna's Gift
Leah's Choice
Redeeming Grace
Johanna's Bridegroom
Rebecca's Christmas Gift
Hannah's Courtship

Visit the Author Profile page at Harlequin.com for more titles.

A Husband
for Mari

Emma Miller

HARLEQUIN® LOVE INSPIRED®

Recycling programs
for this product may
not exist in your area.

™ LOVE INSPIRED BOOKS

ISBN-13: 978-0-373-71934-1

A Husband for Mari

www.Harlequin.com

Printed in U.S.A.

A friend loves at all times...
—*Proverbs* 17:17

Chapter One

Wisconsin

Mari rolled up her grandmother Maryann's red-rooster salt-and-pepper shakers in a stained dish towel and stuffed them into a canvas gym bag. "What time is your boy-friend picking you up?" she asked her soon-to-be-ex roommate.

Darlene pulled her head out of the dark refrigerator, a carton of milk in her hand. There wasn't anything left but condiments, two eggs and the quart of chocolate milk. With the electricity shut off for the past forty-eight hours, Mari wouldn't have touched the milk. Darlene took the cap off and sniffed it. "Twenty minutes." She wrinkled her nose and took a swig. "You want the eggs?"

Mari shook her head. "You take them. I can hardly carry them to Delaware, can I?"

Darlene, thin as a rake handle, features embellished by enough dollar-store makeup for all the participants in a toddlers' beauty pageant, tucked the egg carton into a cardboard box. "Suit yourself." She picked up a green rubber band that had once secured celery and gathered her dyed midnight-black tresses into a pony-tail. "I'm gonna run next door and use the bathroom before Cassie goes to work."

Mari nodded; they'd been using their neighbor's bathroom since the electric was disconnected. Darlene went out the front door, inviting an arctic blast in, and Mari shivered.

She sure hoped it would be warmer in Delaware. Wisconsin winters were brutal. If it wasn't for the kerosene heater, they couldn't have stayed there the past two days. She rewrapped the wool scarf she wore and gazed around. There wasn't anything about the old single-wide trailer with its ratty carpet and water-stained walls that she was going to miss. She had very little to show for eighteen months in Friendly's Mobile Home Park: few belongings and no real friends. She and Darlene had become housemates only because they worked on the same assembly line at the local plant and were both single mothers. They weren't really friends, though. They were just too different.

Feeling the need to do something besides stand there and feel sorry for herself, Mari grabbed a broom and began to sweep the kitchen. She couldn't wash out the refrigerator or wipe down the cabinets, but she could sweep at least. That didn't take water or money, which was a good thing, because she didn't have either. She almost laughed out loud at the thought.

Money had been short since the plant closed and her unemployment ran out. Even shorter than it had been before. Jobs were scarce in the county. Mari had picked and sorted apples, cleaned houses and even tried to sell magazines over the phone. She read the want ads every day, but employment for a woman with an eighth-grade education and few skills was nearly impossible to find.

She pushed her hand deep into her pocket to reassure herself that Sara Yoder's letter was still there and that she hadn't just dreamed it. Sara, an old acquaintance from her former life, was her only option now. If it hadn't been for Sara's encouraging letters and her unsolicited invitation to come stay with her in Delaware, Mari didn't know where she and Zachary would be sleeping.

Mari swallowed hard. She shouldn't dwell on how bad things had gotten, but it was hard not to. First her car had died, and then she couldn't keep up with her cell phone bill. She'd found a few days of work passing out samples of food in a supermarket, but, living in a rural area, without transportation, it was impossible to keep even that pitiful job. Her meager savings went fast; then came the eviction notice.

Mari had tried her best these past few years, but it was time to admit that she was a failure. A bad mistake, poor judgment and a naive view of the world had gone against her. She had nothing but her son now, and she was worried about him. Worried enough to move a thousand miles away.

At nine years old, Zachary was becoming disillusioned with her promises and forced optimism. She was always saying things like "When I find a better job, we'll rent a place where you can have a dog." Or "I know it's a used bike, but maybe next year I'll be able to buy you the new bike that you really wanted for your birthday." Secondhand clothes, thirdhand toys and a trailer with a leaky roof were Zachary's reality. And her bright, eager child was fast becoming moody and temperamental. The boy who'd had so many friends in first and second grade now had to be dragged away from watching old DVD shows on the TV and coaxed to get out of the house to play. In the past month, he'd brought home two detention notices, and most mornings he pretended to have a stomachache or a headache in an attempt to avoid school. She was equally concerned about the envy Zachary had begun to exhibit toward other boys in his class, boys who had name-brand clothing, cell phones and TVs and PlayStations in their bedrooms.

She'd wanted to dismiss Zachary's unhappiness as just a stage that boys went through. A few bad apples in his classroom, a difficult teacher, an ongoing issue with a school bully, would make anyone depressed. But those were all excuses.

Mari knew she had to do something different. She couldn't keep relying on neighbors or roommates to keep an eye on Zachary while she worked odd shifts and weekends. She needed a support system, someone who cared enough about them to see that he got off to school if she had to leave early, someone to be there if he was sick or she had to work late.

Mari had thought she could raise him alone, but she was beginning to realize she couldn't do it. Love wasn't enough. It was her concern for her son that had given her the courage to agree to move to Delaware. She needed to provide for her child, and she needed to give him what he had never had: structure, community and a real home where he wouldn't be ashamed to bring his friends.

Seven Poplars, Delaware, the town that Sara Yoder had moved to, had become a refuge in Mari's mind, the hope of a new beginning. In her dreams, it was a place where she and Zachary could make right what had gone wrong in their lives. Sara had offered her a room in her home and the promise of a job. There would be a tight-knit community to help with Zachary, to watch over him, to teach him right from wrong. And if it meant returning to the life she'd thought she'd left behind forever, that was the sacrifice she would make for her son's sake.

The groan of brakes one street over told Mari that Zachary's bus had entered the trailer park. She put away the broom and began to stack the few bags they had on the couch. Sara had hired a van and driver to take them to Delaware.

The door banged open and Zachary came up the steps and into the trailer, head down, his backpack sagging off one shoulder.

"I hope you had a good last day." She tried to sound as cheerful as she could as she closed the door behind him to keep out the bitter wind. "There's still a couple of things—" She halted midsentence, staring at him. He wasn't wearing a coat. "Zachary? Did you leave your good coat on the bus?" Her heart sank. It wasn't his *good* coat; it was his *only* coat. She'd found it at a resale shop, but it was thick and warm and well made. "Where's your coat?"

He shrugged and looked up at her with that expression that she'd come to know all too well over the past months. "I don't know."

Mari suppressed the urge to raise her voice. "Did you leave it on the bus or at school?" She closed her eyes for a moment. There was no time to go back to school to get his coat before the hired van came for them, and she had no way to get there even if there was.

Zachary dropped his old backpack to the floor. He was wearing a hooded sweatshirt, hood up, but he had to be cold. He had to be frozen.

"I'm sorry about the coat," he muttered, not making eye contact. "But it wasn't all that great. The zipper kept getting stuck." He hesitated and then went on, "It wasn't in my cubby this afternoon. I think one of the guys took it as a joke. I looked for it, but the second bell rang for the buses. I knew I'd be in trouble if I missed my ride home." He swallowed. "I'm sorry, Mom."

She took a breath before she spoke. "It's all right. We'll figure something out." She dropped her hands to her hips and glanced down the hall. "You should see if there's anything left in your room you want to take. Check under the bed. The van will be here for us soon."

Zachary grimaced. "Mom. I don't want to go. I told you that. I won't have any friends there."

And how many do you have here? she thought, but she didn't say it out loud. "You'll make new friends." She forced a smile. "Sara said the kids in the neighborhood are supernice."

He wrinkled his freckled nose, looking so much like his father, with his shaggy brown hair and blue eyes, that she had to push that thought away. Zachary was his own person. He wasn't anything like Ivan, and it was wrong of her to compare them.

"You're talking about Dunkard kids," he said.

"Not Dunkards. That's not a nice word. I'm talking about Amish kids. It's an Amish community. Sara is Amish, and she's—"

"A weirdo," Zachary flung back. "I told you I don't

want to go live with her. I don't even know her. I've seen those people in town. They wear dumb clothes and talk funny."

Mari pulled her son into her arms and held him. He didn't hug her back, but at least he didn't push her away. "It'll be all right," she murmured, pulling back his hood to smooth his hair. "Trust me. You're going to like it there."

"I'll hate it." He choked up as he pressed his face against her. "Please don't make me go. I don't want to live with those weirdos," he sobbed.

"Zachary, what you don't realize," Mari said, fighting her own tears, "is that *we* are those weirdos."

Seven Poplars, Delaware, three days later...

The rhythmic sounds of rain drumming against the windows filtered through Mari's consciousness as she slowly woke in the strange bed. She sighed and rolled onto her back, eyelids flickering, mind trying to identify where she was. Not the trailer. As hard as she'd worked to keep it clean, the mobile home had never smelled this fresh. Green-apple-scented sheets and a soft feather comforter rubbed against her skin. Mari yawned and then smiled.

She wasn't in Wisconsin anymore; she was in Delaware.

There was no snow, but there was rain. They were farther south, and the temperature was warmer here. They'd driven through a winter storm to get to Delaware. The van drivers, a retired Mennonite couple, had been forced to stop not for the one planned night, but two nights because of icy conditions and snow-clogged roads. Mari and Zachary had finally arrived, exhausted, sometime after eleven the previous night.

Mari rubbed her eyes and glanced around the bedroom; there were two tall walnut dressers side by side on one ivory-colored wall and simple wooden pegs on either side of the door for hanging clothing. Simple sheer white curtains hung at the windows. It was a peaceful room, as comfortable as the beds. *An Amish home*, she thought sleepily, as plain and welcoming as her grandmother's house had always been but her uncle's never had. And this one had central heat, she realized as she pushed back the covers and found her way to the chair where she'd laid out her clothes the night before.

She could hear Zachary's steady, rhythmic breathing. She considered waking him, but decided that he needed his sleep more than he needed to be on time for breakfast. Sara had told her that they ate early so that Ellie could be at the schoolhouse on time.

Ten minutes later, face washed and teeth brushed, Mari came down the wide staircase to find Sara in the living room. "Good morning," Mari said.

"I thought you'd sleep in." Sara, short and sturdy and middle-aged, smiled. She was tidy in her blue hand-sewn dress, black stockings and shoes, and white apron. Her crinkly dark hair was pinned up into a sensible bun and covered with a starched, white prayer *kapp*. "But I know the girls will be happy to have you join us for breakfast."

"Should I wake Zachary?" Mari rested her hand on the golden oak post at the foot of the steps.

"Let the child catch up on his sleep. I'll put a plate on the back of the stove for him. What he needs most is plenty of rest first, then pancakes and bacon."

The sound of a saw cutting wood on the other side of the wall startled Mari, and Sara gave a wave of dismissal. "As you can hear, we're in the midst of adding a new wing onto the house. I apologize for the noise this time of the morning, but the boys like to start early so they can get in a full day's work and still get to their chores at home after. Hope they won't wake Zachary."

"It's fine," Mari said. "Once he's asleep, he sleeps hard. Never hears a thing."

"Good. When I bought the house, I thought that it would be big enough," Sara explained, folding her arms across her ample bosom. "But I didn't realize how many young people would want to stay with their matchmaker. I've got a girl living here now, Jerushah, who leaves for her wedding in Virginia in a few days."

Sara was speaking English, for which Mari was grateful. *Deitsch* was the Alemannic dialect brought to America by the Amish and used in most households, but she hadn't spoken *Deitsch* in years, and Zachary didn't understand it at all. That was another adjustment he'd have to make if they remained in the community for any length of time, which she hoped wouldn't be necessary. In light of Zachary's reluctance to make the move to Delaware, the language difference was something she hadn't mentioned. Mari suddenly felt overwhelmed.

What had she been thinking when she'd agreed to come to Seven Poplars? A new school, new customs *and* a different language for her son? How could she expect a nine-year-old, raised in the English world, to adjust to living among the Amish? Even temporarily? Zachary had never lived without modern transportation, electricity, cell phones and television. And he'd never known the restrictions of an Old Order Amish community that largely kept itself separate from Englishers.

But what choice had she had? Apply for state assistance? Take her child into a homeless shelter? She could never blame those mothers who had made that choice, but if it came to that, it would snuff out the last spark of hope inside her. She would know that she was as stupid and worthless as her uncle had accused her of being, the same uncle who had offered to let her come home if she put her baby up for adoption.

Mari mentally shook off her fears. It never did any good to rethink a decision. She would embrace the future, instead of looking backward at her failures. She would make this work, and she would secure a better life for her and her son. "So the job at the butcher shop that you mentioned in your last letter…it's still available?"

"Sure is." Sara's lips tightened into a firm pucker while her eyes sparkled with intelligence and good humor. "Not to worry. I told you that if you came to Delaware, we'd soon straighten out your troubles."

In spite of her jolly appearance, Mari knew that Sara Yoder was a woman who suffered no nonsense. Fiftyish and several times widowed, shrewd Sara was a force to be reckoned with. Like all Amish, her faith was the cornerstone of her life, but she'd been one of the few who'd not condemned Mari when she'd gotten with child out of wedlock and run from her own Amish community.

"Thank you." Mari sighed with relief.

"Enough of that. You'll do me credit. I'm sure of it. Now, come along and have a good breakfast." Sara bustled toward the kitchen, motioning for Mari to follow. "And don't worry about the job. I told Gideon that he'd best not hire anyone to run the front of the store until he'd given you a fair shot at it." She glanced back over her shoulder, her expression clearly revealing how pleased she was herself. "I found the perfect wife for Gideon, and he owes me a favor."

Sara had written that Gideon was looking for someone to serve customers, take orders and deliveries, and act as an assistant manager of his new butcher shop, where he'd be featuring a variety of homemade sausages and scrapples. Sara had explained that he needed someone fluent in English and able to deal easily with telephones and computers, someone who could interact with both Amish and non-Amish. She hadn't mentioned what the wages or hours would be, but Sara had assured her that Gideon would be a fair employer. And, most important, someone would always be at Sara's house to watch over Zachary while she was at work.

The smell of dark-roasted coffee filled the air. Sara's home was a modern Cape Cod and laid out in the English rather than the Amish style, but in keeping with Plain custom, she had replaced the electric lights with propane and kerosene lamps. As Mari walked through the house, she felt herself being pulled back into her childhood, although the homes she'd grown up in were never as nice as this. Sara's house was warm and beautiful, with large windows, shining hardwood floors and comfortable furniture. Sara had apologized that Mari and Zachary had to share a room, but it was larger and nicer than anything either of them had ever slept in. Mari only hoped that someday she could find a way to repay the older woman's kindness.

"There you are!" Ellie declared as they entered the kitchen. "I was hoping to see you before I left for school." Ellie, the vivacious little person Mari had met the previous night, stepped down from a wooden step stool beside the woodstove and carried two thick mugs to the long table that dominated the room. She couldn't have been four feet tall. "How do you like your coffee, Mari?"

"With milk, please," Mari replied, returning Ellie's smile.

It was impossible to resist Ellie's enthusiasm. With her neat little figure, pretty face, sparkling bright blue eyes and golden hair, Ellie was so attractive that Mari suspected that had she been of average height she would have been married with a family rather than teaching school.

Already at the kitchen table was shy and spare Jerusha, the bride-to-be whom Sara had spoken of. "Sit down, sit down," Sara urged. "Ellie has to leave at eight." Sara gestured toward the silent, clean-shaven Amish man at the end of the table. "This is Hiram. He helps out around the place."

Hiram, tall, thin and plain as garden dirt, kept his eyes downcast and mumbled something into his plate, appearing to Mari to be painfully shy rather than standoffish.

Ellie pushed a platter of pancakes in her direction. "Don't mind Hiram. He's not much for talking."

"Shall we take a moment to give thanks?" Sara asked.

Mari bowed her head for the silent prayer that preceded all meals in Amish households. That would be another change for Zachary. Oddly, she felt a touch of regret that she hadn't kept up the custom in her own home.

"Amen," Sara said, signaling the end of the prayer.

And although they were all strangers to her, except for her hostess, Ellie and Sara began and kept up such a good-natured banter that it was impossible for Mari to feel uncomfortable. Again, all the conversation continued in English. Jerushah's barely audible voice bore a Midwestern lilt with a heavy *Deitsch* accent, but Ellie and Sara spoke as if English was their first language. Hiram didn't say anything, but he smiled, nodded and ate steadily.

"You have the buggy hitched?" Sara asked Hiram. "Rain's let up, but it's too cold for Ellie to be walking."

"Ya," Hiram answered. No beard meant that he wasn't married, but Mari couldn't have guessed his age, somewhere between forty and fifty. Hiram's sandy hair was cut in a longish bowl-cut; his nose was prominent and his chin receding. His ears were large and, at the moment, as rooster-comb red as Sara's sugar bowl. "Waiting outside when she's ready," he said between bites of egg.

Hiram had slipped into *Deitsch*, and Mari was pleasantly surprised to realize that she'd understood what he'd just said. Maybe she hadn't forgotten her childhood language.

One bite of the blueberry pancakes and Mari found that she was starving. She polished off a pancake and a slice of bacon, and she was reaching for a hot biscuit when she became aware of the sound of an outer door opening and the rumble of male voices.

"My carpenter crew." Sara slid a second pancake onto Mari's plate. "Better put on a second pot of coffee, Ellie."

Mari suddenly felt self-conscious. She hadn't expected to meet so many people before eight in the morning her first day in Seven Poplars. Now she was glad that she'd chosen a modest navy blue denim jumper, a black turtleneck sweater and black tights from her suitcase. And instead of her normal ponytail, she'd pinned up her hair and tied a blue-and-white kerchief over it. She wasn't attempting to look Amish, but she wanted to make a good impression on Sara's friends and neighbors. Not that she'd ever been one for the immodest dress many English women her age went for; she'd always been a long skirt and T-shirt kind of girl.

Five red-cheeked workmen crowded into the utility room, stomping the mud off their feet; shedding wet coats, hats and gloves; and bringing a blast of the raw weather into the cozy kitchen.

"Hope that coffee's stronger this morning, Sara," one teased in *Deitsch*. "Yesterday's was a little on the weak side. It was hard to get much work out of Thomas." The speaker was another clean-shaven man in his late twenties or early thirties.

"That's James," Sara explained in English. "He's the one charging me an outrageous amount for my addition."

"You want craftsmanship, you have to pay for it," James answered confidently. He strode into the kitchen in his stocking feet, opened a cupboard door, removed a coffee mug and poured himself a cup from the pot on the stove. "We're the best, and you wouldn't be satisfied with anyone else."

"Nothing wrong with Sara's coffee," chimed in a second man, also beardless and speaking English. "James is just used to his sister's. And we all know that Mattie King's coffee will dissolve horseshoe nails." He glanced at Mari with obvious interest as he entered the kitchen. "This must be your new houseguest. Mari, is it?"

"*Ya*, this is my friend Mari." Sara introduced her to the men as they made their way into the kitchen and began to pour themselves cups of coffee. "She and her son, Zachary, will be here with me for a while, so I expect you all to make her feel welcome."

"Pleased to meet you, Mari," James said. The foreman's voice was pleasant, his penetrating eyes strikingly memorable. Mari felt a strange ripple of exhilaration as James's strong face softened into a genuine smile, and he held her gaze for just a fraction of a second longer than was appropriate.

Warmth suffused her throat as Mari offered a stiff nod and a hasty "Good morning," before turning her attention to her unfinished breakfast. She took a piece of the biscuit and brought it to her mouth, then returned it untasted to her plate. She kept her eyes on her pancake, watching the dab of butter slowly melt as she felt the workmen staring at her, no doubt curious about her presence at Sara's. Mari didn't want anyone to get the idea that she'd come to Seven Poplars so Sara could find her a husband. That was the last thing on her mind.

"Thomas would rather drink coffee than pound nails any day," Ellie teased as he took a seat at the table.

"And who wouldn't, if they were honest?" Thomas chuckled. "Pay no attention to her, Mari. Any of these fellows can tell you what a hard worker I am."

"I hope you're not disappointed we've got rain instead of snow this week." James pulled out a chair across from Mari. He unfolded his lean frame into the seat with the grace of a dancer. He wasn't as tall as Thomas. His hair was a lighter shade, and his build was slim rather than broad, but he gave an impression of quiet strength as he moved. "I know you had plenty of snow in Wisconsin."

"I don't mind the rain," Mari heard herself say. "And I definitely appreciate the warmer temperature."

Her comment led to a conversation at the table about the weather, and Mari just sat there listening, wondering why she felt so conspicuous. Everyone was nice; there was no need for her to feel self-conscious.

"Well, I hate to leave good company," Ellie said, getting to her feet. "But if I'm not at school when Samuel's boys get there to start the fire, they won't be able to get in." She tapped the large iron key that hung on a cord around her neck. "They'll be wet enough to swim home." After putting her plate in the sink, she picked up a black lunch box and a thermos off the counter. "Are you ready, Hiram?"

Hiram wiped the last bit of egg from his plate with a portion of biscuit and stuck it into his mouth. "Ready."

Ellie smiled at Mari. "See you after school?"

"Of course. Unless…" Mari glanced back at Sara. "Unless I'm supposed to go to work today."

"Ne," Sara assured her. "Not today. Gideon and Addy have just thrown open their doors, so the pace is still slow. Gideon said tomorrow would be fine. Give you a chance to settle in."

"Going to be working for Gideon and Addy, are you?" James remarked as he added milk to his coffee from a small pitcher on the table.

Mari slowly lifted her gaze. James had nice hands, very clean, his fingers well formed. She raised her gaze higher to find that he was still watching her intently, but it wasn't a predatory gaze. James seemed genuinely friendly rather than coming on to her, as if he was interested in what she had to say. "I hope so." She suddenly felt shy, and she had no idea why. "I don't know a thing about butcher shops."

"You'll pick it up quick." James took a sip of his coffee. "And Gideon is a great guy. He'll make it fun. Don't you think so, Sara?"

Sara looked from James to Mari and then back at James. "I agree." She smiled and took a sip of her coffee. "I think Mari's a fine candidate for all sorts of things."

Chapter Two

The following morning dawned cold and clear. Mari had risen early to help with breakfast and make certain that Zachary was dressed and fed before she left him in the care of Sara for the day. "Wake up, sweetie," she said, shaking him. "Time to rise and shine."

"I want to sleep some more." Zachary tried to roll over, away from her.

"Nope." She put her arm around him. "No can do. I start work this morning."

Zachary rubbed his eyes. "I don't like it here. I want to go home."

Mari ruffled his hair. "We can't, and you know that. We can't go back to Wisconsin because there's no money and nothing to go back to."

"Can't I go with you to work?" He stared up at her with large, sleepy eyes. "I don't know these people."

"You'll be fine." Mari got up and laid out a pair of jeans and a faded flannel shirt for him. "Sara has been good to us, and she's doing everything she can to make this easier. I told you she'd be keeping an eye on you for a few days while I'm at work. As soon as I can, I'll get you enrolled in a new school. You'll make friends, and before you know it, I'll have enough money so that we can move into a place of our own."

Zachary's chin quivered, and he looked as if he was about to burst into tears. "My stomach hurts," he said, not sounding very convincing.

"Don't even try that trick." She'd heard his attempts at malingering before, only to see him devour two bowls of cereal once the school bus went by. "What you need is breakfast. Sara makes great pancakes."

He looked up at her. "I don't want pancakes. I want to go home."

She sighed. "I know this is hard—it's hard for me, too." *Though maybe not for the same reasons*, she thought to herself. She hadn't been prepared for how comfortable she would feel in Sara's house. She leaned down and kissed his forehead. "I need you to try, Zach. Can you do that for me?"

His eyes narrowed. "For how long do I have to try?"

She thought for a moment. She hadn't really given herself a timeline. Had she subconsciously done that on purpose? "Three months," she said off the top of her head. "Promise me that you'll do your best to help me make this work."

He considered. "Three months is a long time. How about one month?"

Mari shook her head. "Not long enough. We have to get our feet back on the ground. I have to earn and save money to get us started again. And even though Sara has been nice enough to let us stay here, I still have to pay for our food and such."

They were both quiet for a second, and then he said, "All right, Mom. Guess I can try."

"Is that a promise?"

"Three months," he said. "But if it doesn't work, if I still hate it, then what?"

Mari walked to a window and stared at the barnyard below. James and his crew had just arrived and they were unloading tools from a wagon. Her gaze fell on James's broad shoulders and lingered. She turned back to Zachary. "I don't know what we'll do then," she answered him honestly. "If we can't make it here in Seven Poplars, I don't know what we'll do." She turned back to him. "But I'll think of something. And that's a promise."

"Okay."

"Good." She smiled at him. "I knew I could count on you. Sara told me that there will be a van here at eight o'clock to pick me up, so we have to hurry. Up and into your clothes, favorite son." She gave him a tickle under his chin.

"I'm your only son!" Giggling, Zachary rolled out of his bed and scrambled for his clothes.

A short time later, Mari was downstairs pouring orange juice at the kitchen table for Zachary. "I'm so glad my new boss is providing transportation to work. I was wondering what I'd do until I could buy a car."

Sara passed the plate of pancakes to Hiram so he could have another helping. "It was Addy's idea that Gideon hire a driver to pick up all his workers and drop them off at the end of the day. Good way to make sure everyone's on time."

"Addy's Gideon's wife," Ellie explained.

Jerushah nodded. "Gideon's wife," she repeated.

Mari buttered a slice of rye toast. "I suppose I expected the Amish employees to walk or come to work by buggy."

"Most of us do use horse and buggy to get around," Sara said. "At least locally."

"Or a push scooter," Ellie put. "I usually ride mine to the school, unless the weather is bad."

"We'd rather keep the horses and buggies off the main roads," Sara explained. "Because of the traffic. But we like horse power, especially for visiting back and forth in our community and for worship services or grocery shopping. Farther than Dover and most people usually hire a driver. And it's reasonable if more than one family shares the price."

"And if the employees drove a horse to Gideon's shop, the animals would have to stand outside all day," Hiram added. "Not good." It was a long speech for him, Mari realized, and as if he'd used up his allotment of words, he reddened, put his head down and concentrated on his third stack of pancakes.

The loud sounds of hammering and sawing drifted from the direction of the addition. "I hear they're at it already," Mari said.

"*Ya.*" Sara added sugar to her coffee. "James is a hard worker."

Zachary slid his plate back. Mari noticed that he'd eaten part of a pancake and pushed his scrambled eggs around, but he hadn't really eaten much. "Can I go watch the men working?" he asked.

"I think you'd better stay in the house out of their way. I'm sure they don't want boys around. Dangerous tools and stuff," Mari explained.

"Oh, let him," Sara suggested gently. "Like as not, they could use some help. There's always something another pair of hands can do, even if it's just fetch and carry. How else is a boy supposed to learn how to do something, if not by watching and learning?"

"Please, Mom?" Zachary begged. "I won't touch anything. Please? There's nothing to do in here. I can't watch a DVD or play a video game. What am I s'posed to do?"

Mari felt her cheeks grow warm. "I'm sorry, Sara," she apologized, meeting her hostess's gaze. "I explained to him about electricity, that you didn't watch television or listen to the radio, but—"

"But it's all new to him," Ellie finished for her.

"So spending time with James's crew might be the best place for him." Sara added a pat of butter to the top of her pancake. "Unless he wants to help me and Jerushah wash clothes." She raised her eyebrows at him.

The look on Zachary's face made it clear he wasn't interested in doing laundry. He turned to his mother. "Please, Mom?"

"If you're certain you won't be a nuisance," she said, relenting. She met her son's gaze. "Promise me that you'll stay back out of the men's way?"

"I will, Mom. Honest." He got to his feet, picked up his plate and carried it to the sink.

"Put what you didn't eat into that pail for the chickens." Sara pointed to a stainless-steel container with a lid sitting just inside the utility room. "Nothing goes to waste here."

"Chickens eat eggs?" Zachary asked. "Yuck. Cannibals."

"Chickens eat most anything," Hiram said. "Even boys if they sit still long enough."

Zachary glanced at him, curious and suspicious at the same time. "Would they?"

"*Ne*, Zachary," Sara assured him with a chuckle. "My chickens would not eat you. I think you are probably too tough to chew."

Zachary laughed, realizing that Hiram had been teasing him, and made a dash for the back door.

"Get your heavy hooded sweatshirt," Mari called after him, making a mental note that she needed to ask Sara where she could buy a decent used coat for him.

"I'm not cold."

"Your hoodie," Mari insisted, rising as she glanced at the clock on the wall. If she wanted to be outside waiting for the van when it came up the lane, she needed to get ready to go. "I don't want you catching cold. Tomorrow or the next day, we'll register you for school."

"Not this week," Zachary protested. "We just got here. I don't want to start a new school in the middle of the week." He stood in the doorway and scowled at her.

"It isn't your decision," Mari reminded him quietly. "I'm the mother." She closed her eyes for a second, suddenly remembering with a sinking feeling that she'd never made arrangements to have his records forwarded. She'd intended to call, but then in all the commotion of packing to leave, it had slipped her mind. She wondered if there would be a phone she could use in the butcher shop. Surely there would be. But what if her new boss didn't want employees using his phone? A lot of places she had worked didn't allow personal calls.

"We're not staying here that long," Zachary said. "So there's no sense in me starting school anywhere." He headed for the back door again. "I'm just going to stay here and build stuff with the men until we go back to Wisconsin." Seconds later, the back door slammed with a bang.

"I apologize for Zachary's behavior," Mari said to Sara and the others at the table. "He's never like this. Honestly." She exhaled, resting one hand on her hip. "At least not often. Excuse me." She turned to follow him.

"Grab a coat on your way, Mari," Sara ordered. "Plenty in the laundry room. If he's going to catch his death, there's no need for you to, as well."

A minute later Mari opened the back door and was hit with a blast of cold air. This might not be Wisconsin, but it was still January and bitter. She was glad she'd taken Sara's advice and taken a barn coat from the assorted outer garments hanging on the wall. She'd also gotten one for Zachary; it would be big on him, but at least it would be warm. There was no way she was going to let him outside in just jeans and a flannel shirt.

Mari crossed the porch and then went down the steps to the sidewalk that ran around the house. She followed it to the new construction, a two-story addition, and caught sight of her son at once. He was standing near a pile of new lumber watching as two men eased a new window into place on the ground floor. "Zachary!" she called.

He turned and hurried across the barnyard. Either he hadn't heard her in the wind or he was pretending he hadn't heard her. She exhaled, debating whether or not to go after him. She didn't have time for this this morning. How was it that children picked the worst times to misbehave?

She was still debating when James came walking toward her.

Suddenly she felt flustered, standing there in the yard with a boy's coat in her hand. "My son..." She lifted the coat and then lowered it. "He's staying here today while I work. Sara's going to keep an eye on him. She said it was okay if he came outside to see what your crew was doing."

"But he forgot his coat." James's kind eyes were now twinkling, as if he and Mari were sharing some sort of private joke between them.

She felt herself relax a little. "Actually, *his* coat is in Wisconsin." She exhaled. "Long story."

James glanced in the direction Zachary had just gone. "What's his name?" He slipped a hammer back into his leather tool belt and smiled at her reassuringly.

She hugged the barn coat against her chest. "Zachary."

James nodded. "Eight or nine?"

"Nine."

"Hard age. Changes are tough for boys. But he'll be fine. He just needs time and patience to adjust."

James's accurate perception of the situation surprised her. "He's a good kid, really," she said. "It's just…a lot for him. For both of us," she amended. "Moving and all."

"And you need him to show more maturity than he's doing right now."

"You must be a father." She looked at him and smiled, then felt awkward. James had no beard. If he had no beard, he was unmarried. If he didn't have a wife, he shouldn't have a child, and she'd just inferred that—

"Nephews," he explained, smoothly ignoring her mistake. "Four of them."

"Nephews," she echoed. "Then you know how boys can be."

He rested a broad hand on his tool belt. "Sometimes boys can try a mother." James stood there for a minute, then said, "Would it be okay if I talked to him? I could take the coat to him. He's got to be freezing." He held out his hand.

"I don't know. It's nice of you to offer, but—" She stopped and started again. "It's just that he doesn't know you."

"But I'm a man." He took the coat from her. "It may be he just needs to talk, one man to another."

The van driver would be here any minute to pick her up for work. She needed to run inside, brush her teeth and grab her lunch box. But she didn't know if she felt right, just leaving Zachary with this man she didn't know very well. Of course she wasn't really leaving him with James. Sara was there and it had been Sara's suggestion that Zachary hang out with the workmen; it had to be safe.

"He'll be fine," James said gently, seeming to know exactly what she was thinking. "Go to work and Zachary will be here waiting for you when you get home with a smile on his face. You'll see."

She met James's gaze, and the strangest thing happened. She believed him.

James watched Mari hurry off into the house before turning back to study the six-over-six wooden-framed window Titus and Menno had just set in place. It looked straight to his eye, but he'd been accused more than once of being a perfectionist. "Best be sure before you nail it in place," he said, picking up a level and tossing it to Menno. "You know Sara. She'd have us take it out again and reset it if it's a sixteenth of an inch off."

Menno grinned. "And she'll be out here with her own level as soon as we leave."

James chuckled and glanced in the direction of the

barn where Mari's boy had gone. "Get the next window in once you're finished. I'll be a few minutes. I might have found a young man to sweep wood shavings and the like."

Leaving the men to continue their work, James crossed the yard to the barn and stepped inside. Out of the wind, with the heat of the animals to warm the space, it was almost comfortable. Light filtered in through a high window, but the stalls remained in shadow. At one end, a wooden partition divided the stalls from the hay and feed storage. His horse, Jericho, stood, ears erect and twitching, watching something of interest near the grain barrel.

James suspected that Zachary was hiding there, but he didn't let on. Instead, he tossed the barn coat Mari had given him on a hay bale and approached the horse. Jericho nuzzled him with his nose, rubbing against James's hand affectionately. "Good boy," he murmured as he stroked the animal's head. How a man could become attached to a motor vehicle, James couldn't imagine. No pickup ever nickered a greeting in the early dawn or ran to its owner looking for a treat.

Jericho nudged him, and James dug into his pocket and came up with a piece of raw carrot. Holding his hand flat, he watched as the gelding daintily nibbled it.

"I didn't know horses liked carrots," Zachary said from the shadows.

"Apples, carrots, even turnips. But Jericho likes sugar cubes most of all." James didn't look in the boy's direction.

Zachary climbed up the half wall of the stall and peered at the bay gelding. He was a little small for his age: brown hair, blue eyes. A nice-looking boy. But he didn't look like Mari, and James couldn't help wondering about his father.

"He's pretty big," Zachary said.

"Just under sixteen hands. He's a Thoroughbred, foaled for racing. But he wasn't fast enough, so he ended up at auction. That's where I bought him."

"They auction off horses?" Zachary stared at the horse.

"They do." James glanced at the boy. He seemed wary, prepared to run if Jericho made any sudden moves. "Have you been around a lot of horses?"

"Not a lot of horses in a trailer park."

"Probably best. Not a lot of pasture in a trailer park." He looked past Zachary to where bales of sweet timothy hay were stacked. "Toss Jericho a section of that hay, will you?"

Zachary didn't move from the stall's half wall. "That his name?"

"It is."

"Horses on TV have better names."

James leaned on the gate. "Such as?"

Zachary thought for a minute. "Lightning. Thunder."

"Thunder. Hmm. Don't know if I'd feel easy hitching a horse named Thunder to my buggy." James glanced Zachary's way. "Nippy out here. You can put that coat on if you want."

"Nah. I'm good." Zachary slid down, broke off a section of the hay bale and stuffed it through the railing. Closing his eyes, the horse chewed contentedly. "He's pretty neat. For a horse. But buggies are dumb. Why don't you buy a car?"

"I had a truck once, but I sold it when I bought Jericho."

Zachary's eyes got big. "You had a truck?"

"A blue Ford F-150 pickup," James answered.

Zachary watched Jericho eat, seeming to be fascinated. "Horses are too slow."

"Depends on how big a hurry you're in, I suppose. Sometimes, you notice things you'd miss if you were in a hurry."

"It must be boring. Being Amish. No video games or Saturday cartoons."

"No, we don't have those things. But we do lots of things for fun. Baseball, fishing, ice-skating, hayrides, family picnics and work frolics."

"What's a work frolic?"

James noticed that while Zachary's voice gave the impression of boredom, his blue eyes sparkled with curiosity. "Well, say someone needs a new barn. Either lightning has struck his old one and burned it down, or a family is starting out on a new farm. A work frolic would be when the whole community pitches in to help build that barn. There might be as many as fifty or more men all working at once."

Zachary frowned. "Sounds like a lot of hard work."

"If you're with friends, all laughing and joking, it is fun. There's nothing like watching a barn rise up from an empty pasture in one day." He smiled. "And then there's all kinds of great food. Fried chicken, shoofly pie, ice cream. And we have games after we eat—tug-of-war, softball, even sack races. Winter is a slow time, because of bad weather. But if you're here in May, you'll see lots of work frolics."

"Oh, we won't be here," Zachary assured him. "We're going back to Wisconsin. I've got friends there. In my old school."

The boy's voice sounded confident, but the expression in his eyes told another story, and James felt a tug of sympathy in his chest. "Must have been rough, leaving all those buddies behind." He leaned on the stall gate. "Coming to a new place where everything is strange. I can see how you wouldn't much care for it."

"I'm not saying this to be mean, but the whole Amish thing?" Zachary said. "It's kinda weird."

James nodded solemnly. "I can see how you'd feel that way. Everybody dressing differently, eating different food."

"The food's not bad."

"I guess your mom's a good cook."

"The best. Great. But Darlene wasn't," Zachary clarified. "She and her daughter lived with us at the trailer until we got evicted. Darlene couldn't even cook mac and cheese out of a box."

James grimaced as much from the idea of Mari and her son being evicted as the thought of macaroni and cheese out of a box. "I don't think I'd enjoy her cooking," he told Zachary.

"Who would?" Warming to his tale, Zachary elaborated. "One time, Mom got this coupon for a free turkey. If you buy enough stuff, the supermarket gives them to everybody. It's not charity or anything."

"No," James agreed. "It wouldn't be if anyone could get one."

"Right. But you had to buy so many groceries and save the receipts. Anyway, Mom got this turkey for Thanksgiving, but she had to work, so Darlene tried to cook it herself." Zachary made a face. "Can you believe she didn't take the guts out? She just stuffed the bird in the oven with the plastic bag of guts inside and ruined it."

James chuckled. "Sounds bad."

"It was." The boy kicked at the bottom rung of the stall rhythmically. "You said you sold your truck. How come they let you have a truck? Mom said Amish drive buggies."

"They do. If you want to be a part of the Amish community and the church, you have to agree to follow the rules. And the rules say no cars and no electricity."

"They think cars and TV are bad?"

James shook his head slowly. "Not necessarily bad, just worldly. Things like electricity link us to the outer world. They take us away too easily from the people and things that mean the most to us."

"So how'd you have a truck? I'd guess you got in big trouble."

"Some but not much." James took his time answering, taking care with the words he chose. "When you become a young man or a young woman in the Amish community, you get to decide how you want to live. Do you want to be Amish, or do you want to join the English world? No one can force you to be Amish, so many Amish young people go out into the world to see if they like it better than this one. That's what I did. I left Seven Poplars and got a job working construction."

"You just packed up and went?"

James nodded again. "I did. My sister begged me not to go. She's older than I am, more like a mom than a sister, because our mother died when I was little."

"No mom. Tough," Zachary said. "My father died, but I never knew him, so I didn't care much."

"Your mom didn't remarry?" James asked.

"Nope. And she doesn't go out with guys like Darlene did. Mom says I'm her guy." He gave a little smirk.

James smiled to himself. He was glad to know that Mari wasn't attached; maybe because he didn't like the idea of her being with someone who clearly hadn't been taking good care of her. He tapped the toe of his boot against the stall. "Listen, I have to get back to work, but I was wondering if you'd be interested in helping us out today. We need somebody to sweep, fetch nails and tools. Stuff like that."

Zachary's eyes narrowed. "Would I get paid?"

"If you do the work, sure. I know you'll be going back to school soon, but—"

"I'm not starting school here," Zachary interrupted. "I tried to tell Mom that."

"You and your mom butt heads a lot?"

"No, not so much. I mean, she's great and all. Really. But when she can find a job, she works a lot. Overtime. Sometimes two jobs at the same time. So a lot of times, I was with babysitters and after-school care. Mom thinks I'm a kid still. She's kind of bossy."

James had to press his lips together to keep from chuckling. "My sister can be like that."

Zachary grimaced. "Girls."

"Hard to understand them sometimes."

"Yeah. But I could probably help you out until Mom figures out we don't belong here."

"I don't know your mother well, but she seems like she cares a lot for you. Like she's trying to do the right thing."

"She's the best. But this was a bad idea, coming here. It's better back in Wisconsin. You're probably nice people and all, but we like cars and TV and electric. I hate it when the electric gets turned off in our trailer."

"Gets turned off?" James asked.

"You know." Zachary frowned. "When you can't pay the bill."

Now it was James's turn to frown. He could imagine how hard it must have been for Mari as a parent, trying to care for her son. "That happen a lot?"

"Mom does her best. Electricity and car insurance are expensive. We make out all right. It's just that Mom lost her job and then we got kicked out of our trailer for not paying. But something will come along. It always does." The boy reached out boldly and patted Jericho's broad back.

They were both quiet for a minute. Sara had told him a little about Mari the week before, that she and her son needed a fresh start, but she hadn't told him that Mari had lost her job and her home. His heart went out to her. He couldn't imagine what it was like for a woman to be alone with no family, no friends, trying to raise a boy properly.

James glanced at Zachary again. "Sounds like what I'm hearing you say is that you might like to earn a little money. And be a help to your mom." He didn't know that the bit of pocket change Zachary might earn would really help Mari's situation, but he did know that even a boy Zachary's age wanted to feel as if he was needed. "Take some of the strain off her?"

"Yeah. That would be good," Zachary agreed.

James crossed his arms over his chest. "And from me and my crew." Again, he was quiet before he went on, "Zachary, I think your mom was pretty upset when she left for work. This move, losing her home and all, has been pretty tough on her. I think maybe she could use a hug from you when she gets home."

"Probably." Zachary looked thoughtful.

"I don't know why you quarreled, but a man's got to show respect to his mother."

Zachary looked up at him. "I'm a boy, not a man."

"But you're old enough to have responsibilities. And it looks to me as though the most important one is to take care of her. Treat her right."

He twisted his mouth thoughtfully. "Guess I should say sorry when she comes home tonight."

"Sounds good to me. So let's shake on it, you doing some work for me." James extended his hand and Zachary took it. Zachary had a firm grip, and James liked that. "But if you're serious about working with my crew, you'd better go put that barn coat on. All of my men come dressed for work, no matter the weather."

"Okay," Zachary agreed. He grabbed the jacket and put it on. "What's your name?"

"James. James Hostetler."

"I'm Zachary. Zachary Troyer."

"Glad to have you on my crew, Zachary." He didn't allow his amusement to show in his expression. *Zachary Troyer*, he mused. *Not so different from us after all.* James had never met a Troyer who wasn't Amish or who didn't have Amish ancestry. Maybe Zachary wasn't as far away from home as he thought.

Chapter Three

When the van dropped Mari off at Sara's after work, she had them let her off at the end of the lane to give herself a couple of minutes to decompress. Her day had been hectic and overwhelming; but she was definitely going to like the job. Gideon and Addy Esch were good people to work for, just as James had said they would be. Gideon laughed and teased her so much, she wasn't always sure how to take him. And Addy had seemed pleased with her, though it was obvious she was going to be the one who would be a stickler for doing things the way she liked them. Still, it had been a fun first day at work, and Mari was looking forward to seeing everyone at the shop the next morning.

Inside Sara's house, Mari found the kitchen a bee-hive of activity. The delicious smells of baked ham, biscuits and gingerbread swirled through the kitchen. Pots steamed and dishes clattered as Sara, Jerushah and Ellie stirred and tasted. Mari was pleasantly surprised to find that Zachary was part of the activity, carefully placing silverware on either side of blue-and-white willow-pattern plates at the large table. And just as James had predicted, he seemed perfectly content.

"How was your day, Zachary?" Mari walked over to the table. She wanted to hug him or at least to ruffle his hair, but she didn't want to embarrass him in front of the others.

"It was good," he said enthusiastically. "I helped work on the addition! I learned how to use a level and how to swing a hammer." He talked faster and faster as he went, as if he had so much so tell her that he was afraid he'd leave something out. "James's hammer was kind of big, but he said he had one at home my size that he'd bring tomorrow. Not a toy hammer. A real one. One that fits better in my hand. A good weight for me, James said. He said I could call him James. That's okay, right? He says that's the way they do it here. Amish people. Kids call adults by their first names."

Mari couldn't resist a big grin. Zachary was so excited and happy that she barely recognized him as the sulky boy who had ridden in the van with her from Wisconsin a few days ago.

"And, oh!" Zachary put down the handful of silverware and dug in his pocket, coming up with a five-dollar bill and some ones. "See. I made money, too." He pushed it into her hand and beamed at her. "For you. You know. To buy us stuff we need."

Tears sprang to Mari's eyes. Zachary could be such a kindhearted boy. She didn't know why she worried so much about him; he really *was* a good kid. "Honey, you earned that money," she said gently, holding it out to him. "It's yours to buy what you want. You could save for a handheld video game or something like that."

He thought for minute and then shook his head. "I

think we better save it for a car, but I can hang on to it for us." He put the money back in his pocket and reached for the silverware, then dropped his hands to his sides.

Mari knew that look on his face. He'd done something wrong. Her heart fell. If Zachary couldn't behave himself when he was at Sara's, she didn't know what she was going to do. She exhaled. "You have something to tell me?" she asked quietly.

He nodded, staring at the floor. But then he looked up at her. "I just wanted to say I was sorry." He spoke so softly that Mari had to lean over to hear him. "I shouldn't have been mean to you this morning. I should have gone and gotten my hoodie when you told me to."

"Oh, Zachary." Mari couldn't help herself. She wrapped her arms around him and hugged him tightly. "I know this is hard, and I'm so proud of you." She kissed the top of his head before letting go of him.

"James says it's important that a man know how to say he's sorry." He picked up the silverware and went back to setting the table.

Mari just stood there for a minute, her heart just a little too full for words.

"What a good boy you are to want to give to your family," Sara pronounced enthusiastically. "I know your mother appreciates it." Then to Mari she said, "Glad to have you home—supper's almost ready. We're all eager to hear about your first day."

"Let me run upstairs and clean up," Mari said as she retreated from the kitchen. "I'll be right back down."

In the room Mari shared with Zachary, she hung up the two new plum-colored aprons bearing the butcher shop's logo. Then she slipped out of her work sneakers and into the only other pair she had.

As Mari tied her shoes, she thought about her day. It had been overwhelming but fun, too. She just hoped she'd be able to live up to Addy's expectations, which were pretty high. But she knew she could do it. She would do whatever she needed to do and learn whatever they wanted her to learn. The other employees were pleasant, including the butchers who worked in the plant, and she thought that dealing with a mix of Amish and English customers would be interesting. She did have experience taking orders because she'd worked at another job several years earlier where she sat at a computer all day selling items advertised on television. But she much preferred working face-to-face with people, and she liked meeting new challenges.

The job would be fine, she assured herself as she ducked into the bathroom to wash her hands and tidy up her hair. She and Zachary had been through a lot of bad stuff, but things were looking up since they moved to Delaware. It had definitely been the right decision; she knew that now. And maybe Zachary was beginning to see that, too. She was so relieved to come home to Sara's and find him smiling instead of sulking in their room. And the idea that he wanted her to have his money and then had apologized for his behavior that morning… It made her heart swell. And it also made her realize that she had some thanking to do, as well.

Once presentable, Mari hurried back downstairs and into the kitchen. "Sara, what can I do to help get supper ready?"

"Could you go outside and hunt down James—you remember which one is James?" Sara arched an eyebrow.

Sara hadn't changed a bit since Mari had known her

in Wisconsin. People said that Sara had more energy
than a March snowstorm. Some called her interfering
and headstrong for a woman, but Mari had always admired her. Now she was once more a widow, but even as
a wife, Sara had been direct and known for speaking her
mind. Very much like Addy seemed to be, Mari thought.
Maybe that was why Addy and her husband spoke so
highly of Sara and respected her opinion.

"I know who James is." Mari suppressed a little
smile. She had no idea what had gotten into her.

"Ask him if he would like to join us for supper. But
not those Swartzentruber rascals. Just James. A new
client will be arriving any moment. We're a household
of women except Zachary, and I don't want him to feel
awkward his first night here. A gaggle of women can
be intimidating to a man."

"Of course we have Hiram," Ellie chimed in. The
little woman was climbing on a three-foot stepladder
to reach a serving plate in the cupboard.

"*Ya*, there's always Hiram," Jerushah said, "but he
doesn't have much to add to the conversation."

"Exactly." Sara smiled. "James said his sister and the
boys were going to her mother-in-law's tonight, so James
will be on his own. Tell him that I'd consider it a favor
if he could put his feet under my table and make Peter
feel at ease. Peter's mother advises me that he's shy, so
I doubt he'll talk much more than Hiram. We need to
make him feel more at ease talking with women. James
will help him relax."

"Whereas," Ellie declared from her perch on the ladder, "Titus and Menno would delight in telling Peter
tall tales of the homely women Sara wants to match
him with."

"Like they did with my prospective husband," Jerushah put in shyly. "They nearly frightened my John into backing out of the arrangement before he'd even met me."

"So no ham for Menno and Titus tonight." Sara gave a firm nod of her head. "They can go home, have cold liver and onions and pester their own mother."

"Like I do sometimes," Zachary chimed in.

The women laughed, and Mari glanced at her son. What had gotten into Zachary? He talked when they were alone together, but he was usually quiet around strangers. Apparently he'd finished setting the table; now he was holding a towel for Ellie. She'd just come down off the ladder to find hot mitts and slide a gigantic pan of gingerbread from the oven.

"So Zachary worked with the men today, I hear," Mari said. "I hope he wasn't any trouble. James said it would be fine, but I don't want to…" She searched for the right words as an image of James came to her and she felt her cheeks grow warm. What on earth was wrong with her, being so silly over some man she didn't even know? Just tired, she supposed. "I just wouldn't want to take advantage of anyone's kindness," she said.

"He was no trouble at all. What this house needs is some active children." Sara went back to the refrigerator and removed pickles and a crockery bowl containing chowchow. "Not only was he no trouble but he was helpful. First he worked outside with the men. Then he came in and made the gingerbread for dessert."

"Zachary made gingerbread?" Mari wanted to pinch herself to make certain she wasn't dreaming. "I didn't know he was interested in cooking."

"Not cooking, Mom," Zachary corrected. "*Baking.* Sara said if I learn to make really good gingerbread, they'll sell it at the shop where you work and I could make money doing that, too."

Ellie carried a pan of gingerbread to a soapstone-topped counter and set it down to cool. "Addy was telling me she thought Sara's gingerbread would be a good seller. I know it's a butcher shop, but they want a couple shelves of baked goods, too."

"We didn't make it from a box," Zachary explained. "I mixed flour and eggs and ginger spice and stuff. It took a long time."

"I can't wait to taste it." Mari offered Ellie a smile of gratitude.

It usually took Zachary a long time to warm up to strangers, but he was acting as though he'd known Ellie for ages. Ellie obviously had a real knack for dealing with children.

Mari heard the sound of a car coming up the driveway, and Sara turned from the stove. "That must be Peter," she said, wiping her hands on her apron. "Ellie, watch that the potatoes don't burn. I'll just go out and welcome him. Mari, can you go fetch James?"

"Going."

"Plenty of coats hanging in the utility room," Sara instructed. "You might as well just save your own for good. On a farm, a sturdy denim is best, anyway."

Mari found a coat and slipped into it. Though the style was certainly utilitarian and obviously Amish, Sara's old coats were warmer than her own. Buttoning up, she dodged Hiram coming in with a bucket of milk and hurried across the back porch.

She walked around the house to find James using a power saw to trim a length of wood. Walking up makeshift steps into the still-open-to-the-elements addition, she called his name, but he couldn't hear her over the loud whine of the power tool. She waited for him to finish the cut and turn off the saw before speaking again. The gas-powered generator was still running, but it was far enough away that the noise wasn't too bad. "James?"

"Oh, hey." He turned toward her and smiled. "Sorry I didn't hear you, Mari. I was just finishing up here."

He said her name correctly—just like Mary. Some people wanted to call her *Maury* because of the way she spelled her name. It was short for Maryann, but she'd never liked that name, so when she started writing the shorter version, as a child, she decided to use an *i* instead of a *y*.

Mari's breath made small clouds of steam, and she pulled the coat tighter around her and suppressed a shiver. The walls and roof cut off some of the wind, but there was no heat. Her ears and nose felt cold, and she wondered how the carpenters could work outside in such bitter weather.

"What can I do for you?" James asked.

And then he smiled at her again, and she immediately became flustered. "Um, I— Sara—" Mari couldn't seem to speak, and she had no idea why. Obviously it had something to do with James, but she didn't understand her reaction. This was so unlike her.

Mari didn't dislike men, but she certainly wasn't in awe of them like other women her age she'd known. She'd learned that a woman who wasn't looking for a boyfriend or a husband found life a lot easier. James was looking at her expectantly, but his expression was curious, not impatient. She glanced around at the half-finished space. There didn't seem to be any of the other workmen there, which made her mission easier since Sara had specified James and not any of the others.

"Sara sent me to ask you if you'd join us for supper," she said in a rush, then went on to explain why Sara was hoping that he'd join them.

James unplugged and wound the power cord for the saw. "I'd be glad to. I'd be having leftovers at home." He noticed her looking at the saw. "You're wondering about the electric saws and such."

She nodded. Sara had a lot more modern conveniences than the Amish community Mari had come from in Wisconsin. Her uncle hadn't even had a real bathroom; they still used an outhouse. Maybe this community was a lot more liberal, she thought.

"Gasoline-powered generators are okay," he explained. "Makes the job go faster. I can build the traditional way when I need to, but Sara wanted this addition done as soon as possible."

Mari took in the size of the structure. "She must be expecting a lot of company. Wanting more bedrooms."

"She's big business in Seven Poplars. Got a waiting list of folks wanting to come and stay and find a spouse." James placed the heavy saw on a stack of lumber and covered it with a tarp. "So how was your first day at the shop?"

"Um. Good." Her mind went blank. She studied him, wondering at his interest in her day. It had been a long time since anyone had asked her about her day.

James Hostetler appeared to be in his late twenties, maybe a little younger than she was. His height was average, maybe five-eleven, not as tall as the Swartzentruber brothers or Thomas. James was lanky, with slender, sinewy hands. His fair German complexion was suntanned, his eyes slightly oval and his hands and wrists calloused from a lifetime of manual labor.

James possessed a typical Amish face, more long than round; light brown feathery hair, very clean; a well-defined nose; and a wide, expressive mouth. He was handsome, though not overly so, with a friendly smile and the intelligent brown eyes she'd noticed on first meeting him. He moved easily, almost boyishly, with a bounce in his step. She didn't know James and she didn't give her trust easily, but she was inclined to like him. He seemed trustworthy, which wasn't a trait she saw often in her world.

Not that she was interested in him in any romantic sort of way. Her life was complicated enough without that. She'd proven with Ivan, Zachary's father, that she didn't have good judgment when it came to choosing a partner. And she had quite enough on her plate without more complications. A man was the last thing she needed.

She found her voice. "My day was good," she said. "Everyone was really nice. There's a lot to learn. I don't know anything about the business, but I want to know everything."

"I'd think Gideon would be an easy boss to work for. And Addy is fair. She speaks her mind and some might fault her for that, but there's not a mean bone in her body." He removed his heavy leather work gloves and shoved them into his coat pockets. "This can't be easy for you, losing your job, your home. Making the move with Zachary and starting over in a new town."

She looked up at him. How did he know about her being evicted from her trailer?

He smiled. "Sorry," he said, seeming to know what she as thinking. "Zachary told me all about it. I hope that's okay. He's a good kid, Mari," he added thoughtfully. "I don't think there's any need to worry about him."

She hesitated. "I wanted to thank you for letting Zachary help you today." She looked down at her sneakers and them up at him again. "And…I don't know what you said to him, but it must have been the right thing. I was afraid he'd be in a funk when I got home, but he's not. In fact, he's great. He seems so…happy. And he apologized to me for his behavior this morning."

The easy smile reached his eyes, lighting them from within and revealing hints of green and gray that she hadn't noticed before. If he'd been a woman, people would have said that they were her best feature. In a man, they were remarkable.

"*Ya*. We kept him pretty busy," James went on. "He carried a lot of coffee, fetched some nails and did some sweeping. We worked on how to drive a nail properly."

"He told me you were going to bring a hammer for him to use. He was really excited about it," she said.

"Good." James nodded his head slowly. "I like your Zachary. You must be very proud of him."

"I am." She smiled. "It wasn't necessary to pay him."

"But it was." He settled his gaze on her. "He earned it. I try to give fair wages for good work."

She pushed her cold hands into the pockets of the coat, trying to warm them. "It was still good of you to take the trouble to make things easier for him. Kids don't like change, and he's had more than enough of it."

"He was no bother. He really wasn't. In fact, it was fun having him with us today. I'm looking forward to spending time with him tomorrow."

James squatted in front of a wooden toolbox on the ground just outside the addition and began to unload his tool belt and fit everything inside. It was an orderly box, his tools clean and well cared for. Mari admired that. She liked order herself, when she could find it in her life.

"Zachary has a quick mind," James continued. "And he's not afraid to get his hands dirty. It's plain to see that you've done a good job with him."

"I try." She stood there for a minute watching him, then realized it was silly for her to just be standing there. She'd passed on Sara's message. There was no reason for her to linger. She put her hands together. "Well, I hope you like ham," she said. "I saw one in the oven. I think Sara and Ellie made enough food for half the county."

"Sometimes it seems like half the county's eating with them. Sara has an endless string of pretty young women and their beaus as dinner guests. She hasn't been in Seven Poplars that long, but she's made a lot of friends here, and there's no doubt she provides a much-needed service."

"Not for me," Mari blurted out, then felt her face flush. "I mean, I'm not here to find a husband. That's not why I came here. We're old friends. From Wisconsin. She's just giving me a hand until I can get settled here in Delaware. I came for the job."

He glanced up from his toolbox. "That's what Zachary told me."

"I'm not married. I'm not even Amish." She felt as if she was babbling. "Not anymore. I was, but—" She pushed her hands deeper into the coat pockets. "Not anymore," she repeated.

He nodded, holding her gaze. There was no judgment in his eyes.

"But you were born to Amish parents."

"Sara told you?"

James shook his head. "A name like Mari Troyer?" He smiled that easy smile of his again. "It's not hard to guess what your background is."

"I left that life a decade ago."

"It's hard, leaving. Hard coming back, too."

"Oh, I'm not... I didn't come to be Amish again. It's not who I am anymore," she added softly, wondering what it was about James that made her feel as if she could stand there in the bitter cold and discuss things she hadn't talked about in years.

"I think the people who raised us, our parents and grandparents and their kin, they're always a part of us, whether we want them to be or not."

"I don't know about that. I guess I'm part of the English world now."

He thought for a moment before speaking. "Has it been kind to you, that world?"

She glanced away. The way he was looking at her made her feel nervous about herself. About things she believed to be true. "Not particularly, but it suits me." She shrugged. "And I can't come back. It's too late." She wrapped her arms around herself, feeling oddly wistful. "Zachary and I are just here for a little while. I've done fine out there. It was just that the plant where I worked closed down. Jobs were hard to come by."

James hefted the heavy toolbox. "I'll be pleased to join you for supper. Mattie, she's my sister, and the kids went to have supper with their *grossmama*. Mattie and her mother-in-law get on like peas in a pod. And Agnes can't get enough of the new twins." He took a few steps and then stopped, obviously waiting for her.

"Your sister has twins?" She caught up with him. "How old?"

"Six weeks last Sunday. William, he's the oldest, and Timothy. They're good babies. It's their big brothers who cause all the fuss in our house."

"How old are they?"

"Roman is three, and Emanuel is twenty-two months."

She couldn't help chuckling. "Bet they're a handful."

"Emanuel takes close watching. Turn your back on that one and he'll be up the chimney or have the cow in the kitchen." They reached the back porch and James carried his toolbox up the steps and set it against the wall of the house. "It will be fine here until morning. Saves Jericho, he's my horse, from hauling it home and back tomorrow." He opened the back door and held it for her.

Mari walked through the doorway into the utility room. Instantly, she was wrapped in the homey smells of food and the sounds of easy conversation and laughter. She slipped out of the coat, hung it on a peg. James did the same and began to wash his hands in a big utility sink.

Mari walked through the doorway, feeling as if she was drawn into the embrace of Sara's warm kitchen.

"Mari, James, this is Peter Heiser." She indicated a thin, beardless man in his early forties sitting at the table. "I know you'll help to make him feel at home here in our community."

"Peter," Mari said as she slid into an empty chair between Ellie and Zachary. "Nice to meet you."

Peter's mouth opened, then closed; then his lips moved, but no words came out. Sweat beaded on his acne-scarred forehead as he nodded in her direction. His pale brown eyes were wide and stunned in appearance, like a frightened deer caught in the headlights of a car. His lips parted again, and something like a croak emerged. Mari expected the poor man to leap up from the table and flee the kitchen at any second.

James came to his rescue, sliding into a chair. "Good to have you with us," he said to Peter. "Everyone. Shall we?" He closed his eyes and slightly inclined his head, a signal for silent grace.

Mari reached for her son's hand under the table. He gripped her fingers, his small hand warm, clinging to hers. She smiled at him reassuringly, and he nodded before closing his eyes and lowering his head in imitation of the men and women around him. Mari did the same.

Mari's head was still bowed when James opened his eyes. She looked so relaxed in prayer. *A brave woman and a good mother,* he thought. He didn't care what she'd said; life couldn't have been easy for her in the English world. It never was for those born into a different one. Not that the Amish lifestyle was a perfect one. Nothing on earth was, he supposed. But it was obvious to him that Mari's struggles must have been more difficult than his own, and he admired her for her pluck and fortitude.

Sara's cheerful urging for someone to pass the ham jolted James from his musing. He caught Peter's gaze and offered him a friendly smile. Poor Peter. No wonder he needed Sara's help to find a wife. The man was obviously terrified of women. Hands trembling, Peter al-

most dropped the plate of meat into Hiram's lap. Hiram
caught it in time, moving faster than James had thought
him capable. Peter went white and his ears reddened.
He was so flabbergasted by his near mishap that he
hadn't even taken a slice of ham for himself. Hiram,
who never missed an opportunity to fill his stomach,
helped himself to two pieces.

"*Ach*, I forgot the butter," Ellie said. She started to
rise, but Mari was quicker.

"I'll get it." Mari moved gracefully to the refrigerator and came back with the butter, offering it to James.

James glanced at Peter and then back at Mari and
wondered if Sara had any notion of matching the two of
them. He doubted it. Sara was good at reading people;
Mari's personality was too strong. Peter needed a gentle
woman, maybe someone a little older than he was, someone who could overlook his social deficiencies. And Mari
had made a point of saying she wasn't here to find a husband. James knew Sara well enough, though, to suspect
that didn't mean anything to her if she set her mind to it.
Sara could be a determined woman, especially when it
came to the idea of there being someone for everyone.
Of course Mari would have to join the church to marry
an Amish man, but that wasn't a far-fetched idea, especially since she had grown up Amish.

Mari took her seat again, murmuring something to
her son. James couldn't hear the boy's reply, but whatever it was, it made his mother smile. A warm expression lit her brown eyes. She was an attractive woman,
probably around his own age. She was rounded rather
than thin and not more than medium height for a woman,
but she gave the appearance of someone much taller.
Her hair was russet brown, her brows dark and arch-

ing over intelligent, almond-shaped eyes. Mari wasn't a flashy beauty like Lilly Hershberger, but James liked Mari's wholesomeness better.

"Pass the ham back to Peter," Ellie instructed.

Peter reached for the platter, his hands shaking.

James glanced at Ellie. Surely Sara wasn't trying to match Peter with Ellie. She was *definitely* too strong to make a wife for Peter. He was very fond of Ellie. He didn't care that she was a little person, but there was no spark between them. And he had no intentions of settling for a wife. Maybe he'd picked up too many English ideas about romance when he was out in their world, but he wanted more than a sensible partner who shared his Amish faith and had reached the age of marriage. He wanted someone to love, a woman who would love him. He wanted a smart, sensible woman who would light up his life. He'd been waiting for that lightning strike, but so far that special person had never crossed his path.

His gaze gravitated to Mari again. At least he didn't *think* he'd met *the one* yet.

It would be good to find the right woman, to move on from being alone to being the head of a family. He wanted a wife and children. He was ready to settle down, but he was a patient man. When the right girl came along, he'd court her properly, treat her tenderly and offer her his head and his heart for a lifetime.

Just as that thought went through his head, Mari met his gaze across the table and she smiled. He got the strangest feeling in the pit of his stomach. When he'd returned to Seven Poplars and been baptized, he'd made the decision to return to the Amish way of life, and that meant marrying an Amish woman. Mari had told him she had no intention of returning to her roots. She'd also said it was too late. But James knew firsthand it was never too late for God's work. Which made him wonder what God had in store for Mari Troyer…and him.

Chapter Four

The following day James pushed open the back door of his old farmhouse and was greeted by the acrid stench of something burning, the fretful cries of a newborn and the combined wailing of two small boys. "Mattie!" he shouted. In the kitchen, smoke was rising from the stovetop in clouds, and from the hall came the shrill blast of a smoke alarm.

James crossed to the gas range and turned off the flame. Using the corner of his coat to protect his hand from the hot metal, he slid the pot over onto a cool burner. "Mattie!" he called. "Everything all right?" The kids continued to cry, but he knew them well enough to know they weren't hurt. He opened a window to let out the smoke, dodged a yellow tabby cat that was fleeing for her life and scooped up twenty-two-month-old Emanuel, who was in hot pursuit of the cat.

The smoke alarm continued to squeal.

With his squirming nephew tucked football-style under one arm, James walked into the living room. Roman, age three, was sitting at the foot of the steps with his eyes shut and his hands over his ears, shrieking. "Roman," James said. "You're fine." Then he called up the stairs. "Mattie? You up there?"

"*Ya.* Just finished feeding the twins!" his sister called from upstairs. Both of the newborns were crying now. "Can you make that smoke alarm stop? I don't know why it went off! I almost had William to sleep!"

"That supper on the stove?" he called above the racket.

"What? Can't hear you!" Mattie shouted back.

James deposited Emanuel on the bottom step beside his sniffling brother and grabbed a broom from the corner of the hall to wave it under the smoke detector and clear the smoke. Some men might remove the battery, just to shut the contraption up, but not James. He'd heard too many tragic tales of smoke detectors without batteries; his family meant too much to him.

"What did you say? I couldn't hear you for that noise!" His sister, scarf askew and face red, appeared at the top of the landing. A fat little baby, six weeks old and as bald as an onion beneath his tight-fitting baby *kapp*, was screeching like a guinea hen.

Like his brothers, James thought. A healthy child with good lungs. The smoke detector finally went silent, and he lowered the broom. "I asked if that was our supper on the stove."

"Not the chicken stew? Did I burn it?" She looked down at the screaming baby in her arms, then at James. "Again? I ruined our supper *again*?"

"Not ruined." James waved her back. "You tend to the twins. I'll see what can be done about the meal."

Just then, Roman yelped, "*Mam!* Emanuel bit me!"

"Emanuel!" Mattie took a step down the staircase.

"I can handle this," James insisted.

She smiled gratefully. "You're a peach."

He picked up the nearest small boy. "Time-out for both of you." He pointed to a small wooden stool. "Three minutes for you, Roman, one for Emanuel." The oldest child started to cry, but James remained firm. "Three minutes." He put the second one on the sofa. "Stay there, Emanuel. If you get down before I say you can, no cookies after supper." Emanuel might have done the biting, but if he knew Roman, the older one, had done something to offend the younger. Easier not to try to figure out who was at fault each time.

James returned to the kitchen, found that most of the smoke had cleared out and closed the window. He removed his coat, hung his black wool hat on a hook by the door and rolled up his sleeves. "All right, Emanuel. You can get off the sofa," he called.

"Can I get up now?" Roman whined.

"Not yet. I'll tell you when." James washed his hands, went to the stove and tasted the stew. The burned taste wasn't awful, but it was there, and there was a thick layer sticking to the bottom of the pot. He carried the offending stew to the sink and poured it into the strainer. As he suspected, the stew in the bottom of the pot was unsalvageable, but large chunks of chicken, the carrots and the onion would be okay with a fresh gravy.

By the time Mattie came downstairs, the two boys were playing peacefully with a miniature horse and wagon, and James had whipped up a batch of corn bread to go with the stew.

Mattie was carrying one of the twins. "William won't go to sleep." She settled into the rocking chair in the corner of the kitchen and watched as he cut potatoes into small chunks, added them to the rescued stew, poured broth from a carton from the pantry into the pot and put the whole thing back onto the stove.

"I didn't get bread made today," Mattie said. "Not even biscuits." She sniffed, searched in her apron pocket, then sniffed again.

James removed a clean handkerchief from his own pocket and handed it to her. "No need crying over burned stew, Mattie. It will be fine. You'll see." He rummaged around on a shelf for some bay leaves, pepper and tarragon. He stirred the spices into the stew and adjusted the flame under it. "Shouldn't take too long to finish, And I've got corn bread in the oven."

"You shouldn't have to do this," Mattie managed, barely holding back tears. "It should be me. I'm not holding up my end."

James crouched down in front of her and patted her hand. "None of that, now. Who took care of me when I was growing up? It's only fair that I repay some of your kindness by helping out. You've got your hands full with four children so close together."

Their mother's death had made Mattie a mother to him when she was nothing but a girl and he was no older than Roman. They were closer than most brothers and sisters. She'd always been there for him, and he valued her wise council. With qualities like that, who cared if Mattie could cook or not?

"You should let me hire a girl to help for a few weeks," he told her.

"Ne." Mattie sighed. "I can't let you spend money so recklessly. I'll be fine."

James shook his head as he rose to his feet. "I never liked this idea, Rupert working away from home. You know he can come and work on my crew any day."

Mattie blew her nose again, threw the apron over her shoulder to cover herself and began to nurse little William again. "He wants to do this, James. Work is good. He's getting overtime every week. We should have enough money to start building our cabin in the spring." She smiled at the thought. "You should be happy. You'll get your house back."

"It's *our* house," he replied. It had never seemed fair to him that his father had willed the house and farm to him. James had given Mattie and Rupert twenty acres across the field to build on, though. Two years ago, when jobs had been scarce in Kent County, Rupert had taken a job in Pennsylvania with a small company that made log-cabin kits and shipped them all over the country. The money was good, better than James could have afforded to pay his brother-in-law, but it meant that Rupert could come home only once a month.

The baby began to make contented sounds, and the tension drained from Mattie's face. She looked up at James. "It's a chance for us. And it won't be long. Once Rupert starts work on our cabin, he won't work away from home any longer. We'll be grateful for a job with you then. And…" She threw him a meaningful glance. "You'll be able to start looking for a wife."

"I will, will I?" His finding a wife was one of Mattie's favorite subjects.

"Lots of nice girls available. You've been back home two years, and you've been accepted into the faith. It's time you thought about settling down ."

When James first returned to Seven Poplars, he'd felt self-conscious when reminded about the period he had spent among the English, but that had passed. Over time, he'd come to believe that his time in the English world had made him a better man. A better Amish man.

"Did you have anyone in particular in mind? For my wife?" he asked, amusement in his voice.

"You know I've always liked Lilly Hershberger. And then there's Jane. She likes you a lot."

"Jane Peachy?" He made a face. "Isn't she a little old for me? She's got to be eighty, at least."

She laughed. "You know perfectly well which Jane I mean. Jane *Stutzman*. She's a good cook. And I know she likes you. I've seen her watching you in church."

He gathered dishes and utensils to set the table for the evening meal. "I met a nice girl this week at Sara's," he said casually.

"*Ya?* Who? Sara's got so many coming and going these days, I lose track. Do we know the family?"

"Her name's Mari Troyer. She's from Wisconsin."

Mattie's eyes narrowed. "Troyer? You don't mean that girl who went English? Sara mentioned her Sunday last. She's going to find her a husband."

"You think?"

"Well, why else would she be staying with the matchmaker?" Mattie asked, sounding as if James was foolish not to have known that. "Of course, first she'll have to join the church. She was never baptized, according to Sara, so it's just a matter of taking the classes with the bishop and making the commitment."

He turned from the stove. "Mari's joining the church?" he asked, trying not to sound too interested; otherwise, his sister would get herself worked up. That wasn't what Mari had said to him. But there had been something in the tone of her voice that had made him think that she wasn't as sure as she wanted him to believe.

Mattie narrowed her eyes suspiciously. "I don't think a girl like that is someone you should court, James. You haven't been back that long."

"Two years." He turned back to the stew.

"It's better if you marry a girl who hasn't been influenced by Englishers. That way you won't be—"

"What?" he asked, staring into the pot and stirring it slowly. "Lured away by fancy cars and HBO?"

"I don't even know what HBO is, but you know what I mean." The baby started to fuss, and Mattie put him on her lap and began to pat his back. "This Mari has lived among the English. She might put ideas in your head to leave again."

James laughed and then frowned. "You think I can be influenced by every pretty English girl I meet?"

"She's pretty, is she?"

"*Ya*. And she has a way about her that's...endearing. One minute she seems confident and the next so unsure of herself," he said as much to himself as his sister. He looked over his shoulder at Mattie. "And she's a good mother."

"She has a *child*?"

"A boy. Nine years old. A man marries a woman with a boy nine years old and he's got an instant helper around the farm," he teased. "Makes sense to me. You know, rather than starting a family from scratch."

"James Hostetler," she admonished. "You're pulling my leg, aren't you?" She cuddled the baby against her. "Well, it's not funny. You've been baptized into the church. If you left again, you'd be lost to us...to me and the children." Mattie shook her head. "It's not a joke, brother."

He went to her and placed a hand on her shoulder.

"I'm not going anywhere, Mattie. And I'm not running off with Mari Troyer." He kissed the top of his sister's head and wondered to himself what the chances were that Sara knew Mari Troyer better than Mari knew herself.

Friday was hectic at the butcher shop, but Mari already thought she was getting a handle on her responsibilities and a good working knowledge of how the scales and cash register worked. She'd even learned a bit about sausage and scrapple making from Gideon. There was a lot she had to learn, but whenever she hit a snag, Addy or Gideon was there to throw her a lifeline. Ending up in Seven Poplars was really quite a turn of events, when she thought about it. Of all the ways she'd tried to imagine finding self-sufficiency, she'd never thought it would be working in an Amish butcher shop and living with an Amish friend.

At five o'clock she hung up her apron and walked out the door feeling as though she'd earned her day's wages. Her only regret was that she had been unable to enroll Zachary in school. The local school secretary had been polite but firm. The school's policy was not to accept a new student without proper documentation, which meant waiting on the school records she'd requested Wednesday.

On the plus side, while at work, Mari had been confident that Sara, Jerushah or James was at the house and watching over her son. But it was unfair to expect them to take responsibility for Zachary when he should be in school. Zachary, however, was more than pleased that he couldn't start yet. And to hear him tell it, he was practically a member of James's crew and on his way to being a journeyman carpenter. As relieved as she was that Zachary was happy, she knew that she had to get him back into class before he fell further behind in his studies.

When the van dropped Mari off at Sara's, the house was quiet. Nothing bubbled on the stove, and the table was not set for the evening meal. Instead of the usual Friday evening supper, Sara was hosting a neighborhood evening meal in a barn that stood behind the stable where she kept her animals. Ellie had pointed it out earlier in the week and explained that Sara had purchased it in the summer for practically nothing because it was about to be torn down at its original location to make room for a development. With the help of friends and neighbors, James's construction crew had dismantled the barn and then rebuilt it on Sara's acreage.

Mari changed out of her work clothing, dressed warmly and followed the pathway through a grassy field to the barn, where light shone from every window. By daylight, it was a postcard-perfect gambrel-roofed building with a metal roof, red siding and jaunty rooster weather vane, but Mari couldn't imagine why Sara would plan a supper in a barn on a cold January evening. Once she pushed open the white wooden door, Mari was immediately reminded of why she should never doubt her friend. Sara's barn was amazing.

Mari gazed around at the interior, taking in the high ceiling, the massive wooden beams and the spotless whitewashed walls. Not only had the inside of the building been insulated, but the old wood floor had been sanded and refinished. Two enormous woodstoves stood in opposite corners, making the main room so warm that she was going to have to take off her coat. And it smelled so good, the scent of burning hickory mixing with one of Sara's cinnamon-and-clove potpourris bubbling on the back of one of the stoves.

The space was a beehive of activity. Men and boys were setting up long tables and arranging chairs while women in Amish *kapps* and starched white aprons carried in large stainless-steel containers and placed them on counters along one wall.

"Mari!" Sara waved to her from the food area. "What do you think of my hospitality barn?"

She laughed. "You can hardly call it a barn. It's beautiful."

This building was nothing like the barns Mari remembered from her childhood; some had smelled of hay and animal feed, but others were not so pleasant. She shivered involuntarily, remembering her uncle's dank and forbidding stable, all shadows, cobwebs and sagging doors and windows. She had spent many mornings and evenings there milking the cows in the semidarkness, and it wasn't a memory that she cared to linger over.

She walked over to where Sara was standing. "When you said you were having dinner in a barn, I wasn't thinking of anything like this. This is terrific." In her memories, her uncle's barn had always been damp and drafty, even in summer. This, in contrast, was a cheerful place, clean and welcoming.

"I'm pleased with how it came together," Sara said, planting her hands on her hips. "If you're looking for Zachary, I saw him just a few minutes ago. If I know Ellie, she's pressed him into service back in the kitchen. Tacos tonight, so there's a lot of prep work."

"There's a *kitchen* in your barn?" Mari asked.

"Right through that doorway." She pointed. "Every hospitality barn needs a kitchen, don't you think? You can go help if you like. I know Ellie needed someone to start the salsa."

"What exactly is a hospitality barn?" Mari hung her coat on a hook on the wall. More Amish were coming into the building now, and two teenage girls were spreading the tables with white tablecloths. "I've never heard of such a thing."

"Made it up myself. I wanted someplace larger than my home where I could get young people together," Sara explained. "For my matchmaking, so that men and women of courting age could meet. Also, our church community needed a safe place to hold youth meetings, singings and frolics. This barn was an answer to our prayers, and it practically fell into my lap. It's more than a hundred years old and is in wonderful shape."

"But the expense of moving the structure." Mari looked around, still in awe. "It couldn't have been cheap."

"A bargain at any price. A lot of Amish communities have problems with their kids being lured into bad habits by the free ways of the English. Even Amish kids need somewhere away from adults to let down their hair, so to speak."

Mari nodded in agreement.

"On Wednesday evenings our local youth group, the Gleaners, meet here. They do game nights, birthday parties and work frolics here, as well. It's good that Amish children learn the value of work and responsibility, but boys have a lot of energy. If we can channel that energy in a positive way, the entire community benefits."

"I didn't realize you were involved in so many projects," Mari said. "You haven't lived here in Seven Poplars that long."

"*Ne*, I haven't, but ours is a close-knit and caring community. I feel like I was called to come here."

"Sure seems nice." Mari smoothed her skirt. "Not anything like where I grew up. I don't think anything had changed in our town in a century."

"Tradition is good." Sara nodded thoughtfully. "It's served our faith well for hundreds of years, but as I see it, we don't live in a vacuum. We have to be open to change when it can be done without endangering our way of life."

Mari had known that Sara, who never had children of her own, had always been interested in kids, but she hadn't realized that her concern went so deep. "And you did all of this for other people's children?"

Sara chuckled. "Not alone. It's really for everyone. My socials are always open to the entire neighborhood. You rarely run into opposition from parents if you have a preacher or bishop present." She lowered her voice. "I'm an obedient member of my church, but some of my ideas do stretch the boundaries of tradition."

Mari nodded. She'd always admired Sara, and now she admired her even more. It was endearing to see that her kindness didn't extend to just old acquaintances who'd fallen on hard times.

Families were filing in, and Mari glanced around, hoping to catch sight of Zachary. So many people who all knew each other was daunting to her. She could imagine how it might be difficult to her son.

The main door swung open again, and James and another man entered, followed closely by Zachary. "Mom!" her son called. He said something to James, who smiled at him and waved him toward her and Sara. Zachary ran to join them. "Hey, Mom." He stopped short and shoved his hands into his pockets.

"I'll be in the kitchen," Sara said, giving Mari a pat on the shoulder. "Through that doorway."

"I'll be in in just a minute to help." Mari turned back to her son. His cheeks were bright red, and she noticed that the cuff of his hoodie was torn. She thought about telling him to run back to the house and grab one of the spare coats from Sara's house, but he looked so happy that she didn't want to seem critical. And to his credit, he was wearing a wool cap pulled down over his ears, like the other boys. She'd thought of Zachary often today, wondering how he was making out. It was a relief to see that he seemed in good spirits.

"I was helping James with the horses." Zachary bounced on the balls of his feet. "He's teaching me how to clean Jericho's hooves. Stones get stuck in there."

"He learns quick, your boy."

Mari looked up to see James walking over to join them. "I hope he isn't being a bother," she said.

James shook his head. "No. Not at all." The warmth of his expression told her that he wasn't simply being polite. "It's a good thing to find a young man who's interested in the care of animals." He raised one shoulder in an easy shrug. "With a horse, feet and legs are everything. They're surprisingly frail for such a large animal. You have to pay close attention to their health."

"Absolutely," she agreed. "My uncle had a horse that had to be put down because a sharp rock caused a hoof infection that spread up the animal's leg."

Zachary looked up at her with obvious admiration

on his face. "You never told me that your uncle had a horse."

A lot I haven't told you, she thought. But she just smiled. There would be time when he was older to tell him the whole story of her life before he became her life. "I'm going into the kitchen to help Sara, Zachary. Want to come along?"

"Can't. James says the men have things to do." He glanced at James again. "I can't believe we're having tacos tonight. I didn't know you people…" Mari saw the hint of a flush creeping up his neck and face as he averted his gaze from James's. "Ate stuff like tacos," he finished, suddenly fascinated by the toe of one of his sneakers.

"I love tacos," James said. "And I like them spicy."

Zachary grinned, his eyes wide with admiration. "Me, too. And lots of sour cream."

James looked to Mari. "I could use Zach's help," he said. "If it's all right with you. I'd like him to meet some other neighborhood boys his age. We'll be right here in the barn."

"Please, Mom," her son begged. "I'll come and help you later. Promise."

James waved to a slender boy with an olive complexion. "'Kota, come here," he called.

'Kota ran to join them. Mari didn't think he was Amish because he had an English haircut, but his plain blue sweater and hand-sewn denim jacket were similar to what the other Amish boys were wearing.

"'Kota is one of Hannah's grandsons," James explained. "'Kota, this is Zachary. Do you think you could take him up to the hayloft? I'd like you two to roll down eight bales of straw. Sara says we're going to play a game later, and we'll need the straw."

'Kota nodded. "Sure. We can do that. Come on, Zach. It's neat up in the loft." The two boys dashed off together.

Mari watched Zachary follow 'Kota up a ladder and climb through a trapdoor overhead. It was all she could do not to call out to him to be careful. "Are you sure that it's safe?" Mari asked James. "Zachary hasn't had any experience in barns."

"Don't worry," James assured her. "Nine-year-old boys climb like squirrels. It comes as natural to them as breathing. 'Kota's a good kid. Zachary will be fine with him."

"Is he Amish?" Mari asked, her gaze still fixed on the now-vacant ladder.

"Mennonite. His mom, Grace, is married to John Hartman, the local veterinarian. You'll like Grace and John. They're good parents. And Zachary needs to make some friends in Seven Poplars."

"You're right," she said. "He does. And I appreciate your help." She smiled at him, thinking how nice it was that he was taking such an interest in Zachary.

She looked at him and he looked at her. He was dressed like all the other Amish men milling around inside Sara's barn, but there was something that made him stand out. "Well," she said, beginning to feel awkward. "Guess I'd better go give Sara a hand in the kitchen."

"*Ya.* Because there will be a lot of hungry people here tonight." He returned her smile. "Me included." He paused and gave her a thoughtful look. "And no need to keep thanking me. I like Zachary, and I've spent enough time with him to already know he's going to be fine.

You really don't need to worry about him. I think you just need to give him time and a little breathing room and he'll settle in just fine."

"Easier said than done." She chuckled. "The *don't worry* part."

"That's what my sister says. She tells me that it's part of the requirements for being a mother. But you need to give yourself some credit. You've done a good job with Zachary. He may kick up his heels at times, like any high-spirited colt, but he's got a level head on his shoulders. He's a son you can be proud of."

"Thank you," she said. "That means more than you can guess." She grimaced. "It's just been the two of us, and sometimes…" She hesitated, surprised that she was talking so easily about her private feelings with James. Again. But oddly, although she'd only known him a few days, James didn't feel like a stranger. He seemed like an old friend. "Sometimes I wonder if I'm being the kind of mother he needs."

"I'm sure you are," James said. "He thinks the world of you." He nodded. "Now I'd best get on with my assignments or Sara will want to know where her straw bales are."

He strode off in the direction of the loft ladder, and Mari found her way back to the well-equipped kitchen. A plump woman that Mari hadn't met was standing at a big gas stove, stirring sizzling ground beef in several cast-iron frying pans. "Reinforcements have arrived," Mari announced to Ellie. It was funny that she'd been tired when she walked to the barn but now she felt so full of energy. And happy to be included in the evening.

"Goot." Ellie was standing on a wooden stool to

reach the counter. "Anna, this is Sara's Mari Troyer. Mari, Anna Mast, one of Hannah's daughters."

"Welcome to Seven Poplars." Anna smiled broadly. She was a big woman with bright red hair tucked under her *kapp* and a smile that warmed Mari to her toes. "Sara told us all about you. We're so glad to have you here. You want to take my place or start making up the salsa?"

"Whatever would help most." Mari liked Anna at once, with her warm expression and laughing eyes. "You're Grace's sister, right?"

"One of them," Anna replied. "Take my spatula and keep this meat from burning. I'll mix up the salsa. Watch me, and you'll know how to do it next time."

"Everyone will be starving," Ellie said.

Jerushah and another young woman who Anna introduced as her sister Rebecca came into the kitchen and began to chop onions and grate cheese. Soon the five of them were laughing and talking in *Deitsch*. Rebecca, a pretty girl a little younger than the rest of them, was as friendly as her sister Anna, and Mari liked her at once, too.

"Oh, don't forget," Rebecca said to Anna after a few minutes, "tomorrow is the coat exchange at *Mam*'s. She'll need help."

"I'll be there." Anna glanced at Mari. "You should come. Sara says you're a good organizer. We could use your help."

"*Ya*, come," Rebecca urged. "We have a good time, and our *mam* really does need extra hands."

"I'd love to." Mari added more fresh ground beef to a frying pan. "But I have to work until noon."

"Perfect," Rebecca said. "I'll pick you up a little after one. It doesn't start until two o'clock, but there's a lot to do there before the moms and grandmothers arrive. You have a son about… What is he? Eight years old?"

"Nine." Mari dumped the pan of cooked ground beef into a strainer.

"They grow like weeds at that age, don't they?" Anna asked. "Anyway, if you have any boots or coats, sweaters or hats that he's outgrown, bring them. We call it a coat exchange, but really it's a clothing exchange for our kids. The whole afternoon is a little crazy, but it's fun. You'll enjoy yourself."

Mari smiled but didn't say anything. She loved the idea of a coat exchange; she just wished she had a coat to contribute.

"And be sure to take something home with you," Rebecca insisted. "If you have a boy, you can always use another winter coat. We do this twice a year, midwinter and summer before school starts."

Anna chuckled. "Mari may not want her Englisher boy wearing an Amish coat. They're warm, and they hold up good, though."

"You can meet our mother and most of the women in Seven Poplars," Rebecca offered. "And you and your son should stay for supper. My sisters will be there, and your son can meet our kids. It will be fun—I promise."

Mari wavered. "I'll be glad to help out, but I'm not sure that your mother will want me to stay for—"

"Our mam?" Anna laughed. "The more at our mother's table, the happier she is."

"She's coming," Rebecca told her sister. Then she glanced at Mari. "You'll have a good time, I promise you. And so will your son."

"All right." Mari gave in with a smile. Everyone was

so nice that she wanted to pinch herself to prove she wasn't dreaming. "Thank you."

"Don't thank us yet," Anna teased. "Wait until you see how much work you've just agreed to."

Chapter Five

The coat swap was every bit as crazy as Anna had warned it would be. Dozens of children ran, climbed, crawled and tumbled through Hannah Yoder's kitchen. Babies cried, clapped their hands and squirmed in their mother's and older siblings' arms. School-age boys in lined denim coats and black wool hats were tugged into the parlor, which held piles of coats of all sizes.

The system was simple enough. People dropped off coats, found ones that fit their children and left. Between helping find sizes, Mari sorted through the trade-ins to see if they needed mending, washing or were too far gone to be used for another boy. Anything that couldn't be worn any longer, she'd been told, would be cut up to be used in rag rugs.

For two hours Mari worked. As fast as coats went out, coats came in, and soon her neat piles of particular sizes weren't so neat anymore. When there was a lull in activity and she found herself alone for a few minutes, she started trying to reestablish the piles according to size. Once she got the piles back in order, she wondered if she ought to go look for Zachary. She hadn't seen him since he'd spied 'Kota when he'd scrambled down out of Rebecca's husband's buggy and ran off after him.

"There you are, Mari!"

Mari looked up from where she kneeled on the floor in the middle of piles of coats to see Rebecca Yoder standing in the doorway, a rosy-cheeked toddler in her arms.

"Have you been stuck in here all this time?"

"No, I grabbed a cup of tea earlier. And I don't mind," Mari assured her. "I like being able to help out."

"I really am glad you decided to join us today."

Mari held a little navy blue quilted jacket in her hands. "It was nice to be invited. I've met so many people that my head is spinning." She chuckled as she folded the garment.

Upon her arrival Mari had met Ruth, Miriam and the youngest of the sisters, Susanna, all redheads like Anna and Rebecca, and all with their mother Hannah's likable disposition. Leah, according to Anna, was serving as a missionary and teacher in Brazil. There was another sister, Johanna, who was expected later.

"So it looks like you're settling in nicely." Rebecca shifted the baby to her hip. "I heard from Addy that you're doing well at the shop."

Mari set the little coat in a growing stack and reached for another. "I really like it there. Everyone has been so pleasant. Not just at work." She glanced up at Rebecca, suddenly feeling very emotional. Sara had written to her about Seven Poplars, but never in her wildest dreams had Mari imagined it would be so nice. "Everywhere I go, people are so kind and welcoming."

"I'm so glad. You know, I saw you talking with James Hostetler last night before you joined us in the kitchen." Rebecca cut her eyes at Mari and smiled as if she knew some secret. "A very handsome, eligible man, that James Hostetler. He seemed very interested in your conversation. Interested in *you*."

Mari picked up another coat off the floor. "James is… very nice. I know him from Sara's. He's building her addition, so we see a lot of each other," she explained, wondering why she felt the need to explain.

"I see." Rebecca drew out the last word.

When Mari dared a glance up at Rebecca, she was still smiling.

Then she gave a wave of dismissal. "Oh, I'm just teasing you, Mari. I didn't mean to embarrass you."

"I…I'm not," Mari managed, still feeling the heat of a blush on her cheeks. "James has been very kind to me…to us. To my son and I. He… I think he'll be a good friend."

"A good friend, yes," Rebecca repeated, her tone still teasing. Her baby began to fuss, and she moved him to her shoulder. "You want me to take over here?"

"No," Mari said. "I'm fine. I'm determined to get these piles in order."

"Okay, well, give me a holler if you need help." She peered into the baby's face. "I think this one is hungry again."

After Rebecca left the room, Mari turned to pick through a pile of coats too worn to be handed out. She came upon a familiar gray hoodie in the pile of blue denim coats. Zachary's hoodie. *What in the world?* He must have slipped in and out again when she'd been in the kitchen having a quick cup of tea with the Yoders when she first arrived. She was holding it up, wondering what he was wearing, when she heard a familiar male voice.

"Hey! I didn't expect to see you here."

She looked up to see James standing in the doorway holding the hand of a small boy in a black hat and blue denim jacket identical to his. Her first thought was one of fear. He must have passed Rebecca in the hallway. Had he overheard them talking about him? "James."

"My nephew Roman," he introduced him, pointing down at the little boy.

If he'd heard any of her conversation with Rebecca, he didn't give any indication, which made Mari sigh with relief. Not that she'd said anything wrong or inappropriate, she just... *You just what?* She looked down at the little boy.

The child eyed her suspiciously.

"Roman, here, is in need of a larger coat than the one he has."

The boy ducked behind James's legs and buried his face in his uncle's trousers.

"Hello, Roman." Mari rose from the floor. "Did you come to find a new coat?"

James shook his head. "He doesn't understand English yet." He quickly translated for the child. Roman peeked around James's legs at her and buried his face again.

"Ne," Roman murmured.

"Ya," James corrected. Then he returned his attention to Mari. "My sister's twins were fussy today, so I was elected to coat detail," he explained. "Do you think you can help us? We're not trading in this one, because there are three more boys younger than Roman, but my sister sent a pile of mittens she knitted. They were gone before I got through the kitchen." He reached behind him, scooped up the boy and tucked him under his arm.

"Of course if we can't find something that will fit him," James said, switching back to *Deitsch*, "we'll just trade him for one of the bigger boys outside who comes with his own coat that fits." James didn't crack a smile and appeared perfectly serious.

Roman began to giggle, James broke into a grin, and Mari found herself chuckling with them.

"I'm sure we won't have to go that far," she said in *Deitsch* so Roman would understand her. She was amazed by how easily the language was coming back to her. "We can find something that will fit him. We probably have more of the smaller coats left than the ones for the older boys."

"So long as I go home with one boy and one coat," James said. "Otherwise, I'll have some explaining to do." He hesitated and then said, "Your *Deitsch* is good. I'd never have suspected you'd been away so long."

"Thank you." Mari turned away, suddenly feeling shy and having no idea why. "So...let's see what we can find."

Finding a coat for Roman at the coat exchange proved more difficult than James expected. Because all of the jackets had been handmade, nothing was marked with sizes. Some were too long, some too short. And every one of them looked just like the others to him until he got it on his nephew. And then once he found one that fit, the trouble was finding one that would be acceptable to his sister. One had been poorly patched, and others were badly worn or not sewn as neatly as Mattie would have liked. The denim coats were fastened with snaps rather than buttons, and he'd been instructed not to bring a garment home that had missing or broken snaps. Most of the jackets were lined, but in different material and padding, and not all were as warm as what James wanted for Roman.

"He's an outside boy and rough on his clothing," James explained to Mari in *Deitsch*. Roman beamed. "He needs something that will protect him from the cold and something that will hold up. Mattie wasn't sure that she could trust me to pick out the right coat, but I told her I could. So my reputation is pretty much on the line here."

"Not to worry," Mari promised as she dug through a pile of coats. "We'll find one here somewhere and Roman will go home as warm as toast."

Roman wasn't happy about actually trying on the coats, and he was soon squirming and whining in protest. James could understand the boy's reaction. Unlike his sisters, he'd never had the patience to stand still while his *mam* measured him for new clothing or had him try on new garments she'd made.

"There must be something suitable here," James said to Mari, looking through another pile. "I promised Mattie that I'd find him something that she wouldn't be ashamed for him to wear to Sunday worship. She was hoping to make him a new coat, but the twins keep her pretty busy."

"Twin newborns?" Mari's smile lit her dark eyes. "I'd think they would."

James decided she had a nice smile. "You should hear William, the older of the twins. He has a set of lungs on him."

"Bless her. I can't imagine how she does it. I was at my wit's end with Zachary when he was a baby. I think raising a monkey would be easier than twins."

She was a woman with a sense of humor, and he liked that. He really hoped that she and Zachary would decide to stay in Seven Poplars because they would be a welcome addition to the community. And he couldn't help thinking how easily she seemed to fit in among them. He'd seen it at Sara's house and then at the dinner the previous night, too. Maybe she just needed a little encouragement and support from everyone.

"How about this one?" Mari held up another coat. "This would be fine to wear to worship."

"Let's hope it fits." He reached for it. "Are you coming tomorrow?"

"Coming where?" She looked up at him, another coat now in her hand.

He went down on one knee to wrestle Roman into the coat. "To worship. With Sara, Ellie and the others? Last Sunday was visiting Sunday, so we have worship tomorrow."

Mari's mouth tightened, and she visibly paled. "No," she said, shaking her head. "I'm not coming."

"That's too bad." He realized he had made her uncomfortable, and that hadn't been his intention. "We've got a good preacher. Caleb. He's a young man, but he knows the word of God."

She glanced at the coat in her hands, then up at him. "You might as well know right off, James, that I don't go to church anymore," she said quietly. "I haven't been to an Amish service since I left my uncle's farm when I was eighteen."

"Do you mind if I ask why not? Sara said you were raised in the faith," he said.

When he met Mari's gaze, he saw that her eyes suddenly glistened, and he wished he'd chosen his words more carefully. She looked as if she might cry. He released his hold on Roman, and the boy got down on his knees and crawled under a chair to pick up a wooden rabbit that some other child must have left behind in the parlor.

James sat down on a wooden stool and looked at Mari. He was already beginning to think of her as a friend. A very good friend. And he disliked the idea of upsetting her. "I'm sorry," he said. "I didn't mean to pry."

"No, it's all right." She swallowed, obviously trying to regain her composure.

He was quiet for a moment. Logic told him to change the conversation, but there was something about the look on her face that made him think that wasn't what he was supposed to do. It wasn't the Amish way to talk about God leading a person to do something or say something, but it *was* the Amish way to respond to such callings. "Do you miss it?" he asked softly in English, knowing she did. He could see it in her eyes.

"Sometimes," she admitted, meeting his gaze for a moment, then looking away. She hesitated and then went on in English, "It's hard to explain, James. Why I left the church. I don't think I've lost my faith in God, but…I think He turned away from me."

Someone or something had hurt her badly to make her say such a thing, and James instantly felt protective of her. His first instinct was to get up and go to her and put his arm around her. That wouldn't have been appropriate, of course. So he stayed where he was. "I don't think God ever turns away from us, Mari."

"It felt like it at the time." She hugged the little coat to her chest. "I wasn't welcome in my family's home anymore."

"Were you placed under the *bann*?" he asked.

Mari shook her head. "No. I left the morning of the day I was supposed to be baptized." Her lower lip quivered. Suddenly she seemed younger, more vulnerable. But she raised her chin and looked directly into his eyes. "I couldn't go through with it, and so I ran away."

"To the English world," he said, remembering so vividly the day he'd done the same thing. Only he'd been fortunate enough to not have to leave in the cover of darkness as many Amish did. His family had been there in the barnyard to say goodbye and to hug him and wish him well and encourage him to come home as often as he wished.

"Yes." A tear welled in the inner corner of her left eye, and she dashed it away.

"And you never went home again? Later, after the fuss of your leaving had died down?"

"I went to my uncle once, when I knew I was expecting." She didn't look at him when she said the words. "He said I would have to give up my baby in order to come home, so I didn't go back after that."

"Your brothers and sisters? Did they feel the same way?"

"My sisters were married and gone. I don't know where, but they were older, and we were never close. My brother...he died."

"I'm so sorry," he said, finding himself feeling the grief that clouded her beautiful eyes. "If you weren't baptized, there was no reason for them to treat you that way. Our faith gives each person the choice of baptism. Our church doesn't shun the ones who leave."

"Ours didn't, either. But my aunt and uncle were...

not very understanding. He was a deacon, and he felt I had shamed him in front of the congregation."

They were both quiet for a long few moments and James knew he should let the conversation go, that he should take a coat and walk away, but he couldn't leave Mari like this. "Were you happy out there? Among the Englishers?"

"Yes," she answered too quickly. She set the coat in her arms aside and picked up another. "Well, sometimes…most of the time."

"But lonely," he said, seeing it in her face. "I know. I found that out for myself. I left Seven Poplars when I was twenty."

"You did?" She looked up at him with surprise. "That's hard to believe. You seem so…so Amish."

He had to laugh at that.

"You know what I mean." She smiled and dropped to sit on the edge of a chair, facing him. "You seem so content. So happy with your life."

"I am now." He held her gaze, smiling. "I can't believe Zachary didn't tell you I was English for a while."

"Zachary knows?" Again he could tell she was surprised. "He never said a word, that little rascal. How long were you gone?"

"About six years."

She was quiet for a moment and then she looked at him. "Can I ask you something?"

"Of course."

She met his gaze. "What made you come back?"

"Realizing this is where I belong. It's a good life for some out there. But it wasn't for me. I learned a lot out there about people, about book stuff we don't teach in our schools, but I think that the most important thing

I learned was that I belong here. Seven Poplars is my home."

"How long have you been back?" she asked. She held up a hand. "Sorry. I don't mean to pry."

"It's not prying. It's common knowledge in Seven Poplars. I've been back two years."

"And you've joined the church?"

He nodded. "*Ya.* First thing I did when I moved home. And it's brought me peace. Peace I never knew before."

"I'm glad for you," she answered, and he could tell she was being sincere. "But not everyone is meant for the life apart from the world like this."

"That's true," he agreed.

She met his gaze again, and he wanted to ask her how sure she was that she was one of those people, but the same feeling that he had a few minutes earlier telling him to press on told him to let it go. So he did. Instead, he reached for Roman, who was crawling past him with the toy rabbit. "There you are!" he cried, lifting the boy into his lap and tickling him.

"Try this one on him," Mari said, rising off the chair. She held up a small coat with neat stitching and a mended tear on the right cuff.

"I don't know about the mend," James said and then smiled. "Maybe Mattie was right. Maybe this job is too big for me."

"Absolutely not." Mari put the coat aside. "I think the ones in the baby room are too small for him, but..." She picked up a garment that had fallen between the chairs. "Let's try this."

To James's relief, the coat she handed him was only slightly big. "That should do it," he said, slipping it over his nephew's shoulders. The coat was sewn with stitches almost too small to see. The lining was quilted, and there were elastic cuffs inside the sleeves that would keep the winter wind from blowing up a boy's arms. Roman wiggled and shifted his feet, wanting to get back to his game with the rabbit, but Mari insisted on fastening all the snaps to make certain none were missing or broken.

"Nice fit" came a woman's voice from the doorway. "Be sure you grab one of those knit caps on the windowsill."

James looked over to see several small hats lying there. "Thank you, Hannah. I think we've found a coat that Mattie will like."

"And there's a little room for him to grow," Mari pointed out.

"He does that," James said. "I've tried putting him under the kitchen table and telling him not to, but every time I turn my back on Roman, he shoots up another inch or two."

The boy giggled.

"The fit looks perfect to me," Hannah said. "Find one to fit any better and a boy will outgrow it before he gets through the kitchen doorway." She shifted a fat-cheeked baby from one hip to the other. "I think Roman is our last customer." She glanced at the remaining coats. "At least we didn't come up short like last year. Ellie can take these spares to the school to see if anyone there can use one."

James helped Roman out of the coat, and as he did, he noticed the outline of a bee stitched into the inside at the back of the collar. "Look, Roman," he said to the boy. "Your new coat has a bee in it."

Roman laughed and scrambled to retrieve the toy rabbit.

"Johanna's work," Hannah explained. "She raises bees, and she sews a bee into her boys' coats. Our Johanna is an accomplished seamstress. Have you met her yet?" she asked Mari. Mari shook her head. "Well, you will because she and the children are coming for supper. Rebecca and Anna tell me that you're staying to eat with us, too. I'm so pleased to have you."

"That's not necessary," Mari replied. "You have a houseful already."

"*Ach*, the more at my table the happier my husband will be. He had no children of his own until he married me and inherited my lot. Now to see him, you'd think he fathered them all. And he spoils the grandchildren rotten."

"And you'd have to be foolish to turn down Hannah's invitation," James warned. "Everyone knows what a fine cook she is."

"Flattery will get you nowhere, James Hostetler," Hannah teased.

The baby popped a thumb into its mouth. James wasn't sure if it was a boy or a girl. "Not even an invitation to supper?" he said to Hannah.

She chuckled. "I was going to ask you anyway. Albert wants to ask your advice about a new shelter for the alpacas. My husband is mad for his alpacas," she explained to Mari. "We sell the fleece, and some girls in the neighborhood are learning to spin and weave the wool into yarn."

"I've heard that alpaca fleece brings a good price," Mari said. "Some of the expensive shops in Wisconsin sell alpaca hats and sweaters."

"Ya," Hannah agreed. "The fleece more than pays for the keep of the alpacas."

"Hannah will tell you that alpacas are Albert's hobby," James said, "but listen to her. She is fond of them, as well."

"I am," Hannah agreed. "Women who become skilled spinners and weavers can bring in extra money without leaving their homes. It helps our families and our community." She smiled at Mari. "Johanna teaches classes in her home one evening a week if you're interested in learning. Our Grace is picking up the skill quickly. I think you would like Grace. Her son, 'Kota, and your boy seem to have hit it off."

"Oh, my Zachary." Mari flushed. "I found his hoodie here in the pile of coats. I'm afraid he took one of the denim ones. We didn't bring a coat to contribute, so I can't—"

"Of course you can," Hannah scoffed, interrupting her. "What mother can't use another coat for her child? Look at what we have left. You're doing us a favor if you let Zachary keep it."

Mari appeared hesitant. "That's kind of you, but I wouldn't feel right about it."

"Why not?" Hannah asked. "You can always use it for him to play in. Zachary must have wanted to wear it or he wouldn't have traded it for his own."

"I suppose you're right," Mari agreed reluctantly.

"You can ask him at supper," Hannah said with a smile. "I promise you he'll be on time for that. Because if there's one thing boys like more than playing, it's eating. 'Kota's staying to eat with us, as well as Johanna's J.J. and Jonah. They're close in age to your Zachary." She turned to go. "He'll fit in here like a pea in a pod."

Chapter Six

The family supper was at six and lasted until nearly eight o'clock. Mari enjoyed the meal, and—to her surprise—she had felt at ease with the Yoder family. She fit in as easily as, to borrow Hannah's expression, a pea in a pod. The huge kitchen had been warm and inviting; the food had been delicious. And she'd eaten far too much. What she didn't understand was how or why, exactly, she'd ended up agreeing to ride home to Sara's with James in his buggy.

"*Ach*, not to worry," Hannah had said, patting her on the forearm as they made their way to the utility room where everyone had left their coats and boots. "Everything is proper. No one will think anything of it. Your son is with you. And Johanna's J.J. and Jonah. James is dropping them off with their father. Anyway, James insisted he drive you. It's too cold out for you and Zachary to walk."

Anna pushed a wicker basket of leftovers into Mari's hand. "*Schnitz und knepp. Mam*'s dried-apple dumplings. Sara's favorite. And there's a tub of German potato salad and some roast duck with stuffing. For the

Sabbath." Anna's round face creased with good humor. "We don't cook on Sundays, and I know Sara always has company stopping in after church."

"Thank you so much," Mari said. She supposed it was a good thing she wasn't walking home. It was at least half a mile to Sara's, and both houses had long driveways.

"Sundays are a day of rest for the women, *ya*? It must have been a woman long ago who whispered that rule in her husband's ear. No work on the Sabbath." Anna chuckled as she scooped up an adorable little red-haired girl and wiped jam off her chin and planted a kiss on the child's rosy cheek. "My Rose," she said. Rose giggled and squirmed. "This one's ready for bedtime."

"How many children do you have?" Mari asked.

"There is Rose and Baby Naomi, little Mae and our Lori Ann. Then the boys Peter and Rudy. They're twins and rascals both. My dear Samuel brought me five of them from his first marriage, but I never remember which five they are." She leaned close and hugged Mari. "I'm so glad you stayed for supper, and so happy that you're staying with Cousin Sara. We all adore her, and we can see why she speaks of you so highly."

Somehow, amid the laughter and embraces Mari said her goodbyes, found her own coat and made her way to the kitchen door, where James and Zachary, now wearing identical blue denim coats, were standing amid a gaggle of boys.

Mari knew 'Kota and remembered that two of the boys belonged to Johanna, but she was at a loss as to who the others were. Zachary, however, seemed to know them all, and there was a great deal of teasing, pushing and shouted plans for some future enterprise as her son made his way out onto the back porch.

From the porch, Mari stepped outside into a brisk and bitter night. Since there were no artificial lights on the house or barn and there was no moon, the flashing battery lights on the buggy seemed startlingly bright. There was no heat inside the vehicle, but Mari knew the exterior would cut the wind. It had been a long time since she'd ridden in a buggy, and she wasn't sure whether it would bring back welcome or unwelcome memories from her childhood.

James walked around to the back and opened the door for the boys. 'Kota, J.J., Jonas and Zachary all piled in to sit on the facing backseats. James untied his horse from the hitching rail, wrapped the lines around a knob on the dash and followed Mari around to the far side of the buggy.

Mari quickened her step. The ground was frozen under her feet, and the cold seemed to leach up through the soles of her sneakers. She took hold of the buggy and started to climb up into the front seat, but she was in too much of a hurry. Her foot missed the metal bar that served as a step. She slipped and fell back, stumbling as she attempted to keep her balance.

James's strong hands closed around her waist and steadied her. "Sorry," he said. "I should have helped you up."

She looked over her shoulder at him, and he held her gaze for a split second. She remembered what Rebecca had said earlier in the day about him being interested in her. Surely Rebecca was mistaken.

"No, it was my fault," she said. His touch made her feel more off balance than her awkward attempt to climb into the buggy. Her hand tightened on the grab bar, and he boosted her up. She scrambled up into the seat. "Got it," she said. "Thanks."

He circled the front of the horse and buggy and climbed into the driver's seat. "Night!" he called to Albert and Hannah and the boys who were watching from the porch.

"This is cool," Zachary said from the darkness in the back of the buggy. One of the other kids said something in *Deitsch*, and they all giggled, including her son. Mari wondered if he'd understood what had been said or if he was just pretending he did.

A whip stood by James's left hand, but he never touched it. He made a low clicking sound, and the horse started off, first at a walk and then at a trot. The wheels made a familiar sound on the frozen ground, and the leather creaked. Mari closed her eyes and her mind returned to earlier times. Luckily, it was only good memories that came to her: memories of being cozy in the back of the family buggy with her cousins, memories of a feeling of belonging and safety.

They were halfway down the lane when James spoke. "Here. Put this over your lap. You boys warm enough back there?" he asked as he passed her a heavy woolen blanket. "Blankets under the seat."

"Wait!" Mari said, suddenly remembering how many boys had climbed into the back. "Did you forget Roman?"

James laughed. "*Ne*, Grace drove him home earlier. Mattie likes to have the boys in bed early. Grace had stopped to see if 'Kota was behaving himself. She was on the way to help her husband, John, with a late check on a horse. She's going to pick her boy up from Johanna's when they're finished."

Mari thought about how many times she'd struggled

to find good child care for Zachary and the jobs and overtime she'd had to refuse because there was no one. "Must be nice to have so many willing babysitters," she said wistfully.

"Isn't that what family and friends are for?"

She glanced at James as they pulled out onto the road, surprised by how comfortable she felt with him. How at ease she'd felt all day, really. She was glad she'd come today.

"Glad you came today," James said.

She laughed out loud at the fact that the both of them had thought the same thing at the same time.

"What?" he asked, looking at her. "What's so funny?"

She shook her head and glanced away, feeling a blush creep across her cheeks. The longer she knew him, the more handsome he seemed to get. "It's nothing."

He smiled down at her. "I was just saying, I'm glad you came and I'm also glad you agreed to ride home with me, too. Otherwise, I imagine Hannah would have put some eligible unmarried girl in my buggy seat."

She lifted her brows. "Hannah's trying to fix you up? I thought Sara was the matchmaker in Seven Poplars."

"I think every woman over the age of sixteen sees herself as a bit of a matchmaker," he joked. "Half the women in my church are scheming to match me up with one of their sisters or daughters or cousins. Mattie won't stop bringing up the subject of my marriage to a nice girl. She's already picked out the bride."

Mari felt a sudden sense of disappointment and she didn't know why. "Someone in Seven Poplars?"

"*Ya.* And there's nothing wrong with the girl. I just don't know if she's the right one, and I refuse to let Mattie push me into courting someone." He shrugged.

"I know it's not what's expected, but…" He sounded sheepish. "This probably sounds silly, but I'm looking for love, Mari. Real love."

Mari steadied herself as the buggy rolled over a pothole, trying to keep from brushing up against him. "Have I met this girl your sister likes for you?"

"She was at Sara's shindig last night. Lilly Hershberger. Curly blond hair. Dimples. Pretty girl. Smart. She'll make someone a good wife."

Noisy chatter came from the back of the buggy. The boys were obviously occupied with their own concerns, and Mari felt free to talk without fear of being overheard. "How does Lilly feel about you?"

James considered. "She's nice enough to me, but then Lilly's nice to everyone. My sister keeps mentioning Jane Stutzman to throw me off, but I know it's Lilly she wants me to walk out with."

He was talking to Mari as if she were a good friend. A confidant. Rebecca had obviously been mistaken when she said he'd been interested in her. James obviously saw her as a friend he could talk to. Why else would he bring up courting another girl? "So what are you going to do?"

"I don't know what to do. Do I give in to my sister? Maybe I should ask to take Lilly home from the next get-together. That's the way it usually starts here," he explained. "I ask one of her cousins or her friends if she'd be willing to ride home with me. They ask and then let me know. That way no one is embarrassed if she's not willing. If she is, I don't really have to say anything to her. It's just understood. We socialize with the rest of the group, and then when it's over, I ask her if she's ready to leave."

"So you don't take her to the frolic, like the English would. You just drive her home?"

"Exactly."

"And do you need a chaperone or do you have an open buggy? Most of the young men back in Wisconsin drove a courting buggy for their dates. In a closed buggy, like this, they'd have to have someone with them."

James shook his head as he turned the horse into a driveway on the left side of the road. "An open buggy or a chaperone isn't necessary, not if I'm just driving a girl home. If we were gone all day or went to Lancaster, maybe. But Bishop Atlee is reasonable."

"I guess our church was stricter," Mari said, liking the idea that she could bring up the life she used to have among the Amish and not feel uncomfortable. In the English world, she'd never talked about her life among the Amish.

She glanced out over the ears of James's horse; she could see the amber glow of lights, and as the horse trotted up the lane, the dim outline of Johanna's farmhouse became visible. There were no curtains at the windows, and the shades were still up. The house looked warm and inviting. James called over his shoulder, "Here we are, boys. And there's your *dat* at the door."

Home, thought Mari. As she watched the boys clamber out of the back of the buggy, she couldn't helping wishing the house was hers and Zachary's, and that she was coming home. The man in the doorway was a shadow, but he wasn't the attraction. And for an instant she was seized by the old desire to belong somewhere.

She glanced at James and felt a heaviness in her chest that she couldn't identify. A longing. She glanced back at the house.

Coming home. It was a dream that she cherished, a dream she didn't know would ever come true.

"Are you sure you won't come with us?" Ellie asked Mari the next morning. She and Sara were dressed for church, and Hiram had brought the buggy around to drive them all to Johanna and Roland's place. "You know that everyone would be happy to have you."

Mari nibbled on her lower lip in indecision. All night she'd wrestled with the dilemma of what to do about church. Sara and Ellie wanted her to go. And James had asked her to go, too. In their letters back and forth Sara had mentioned church, and relayed Bishop Atlee's invitation to attend, but Mari hadn't committed because she honestly hadn't known how she felt about it. Now that she was here, a part of her wanted to go, but part of her was afraid. What if she liked it? She'd told Zachary they would be in Seven Poplars until they got their feet back under them. They'd never really discussed staying. She hadn't even considered it… Had she?

She hesitated and then said to Sara, "I don't know. I'm not sure Zachary would want to—"

"I'll go!" Zachary declared excitedly. He was standing at the kitchen sink putting silverware in a pan of soapy water to be washed come Monday. When he turned so quickly to them, he sprayed little drops of water.

"You'll go to church?" Mari asked in surprise.

"J.J. asked me to come. He said we just have to be quiet for a little while. He said it's fun and his aunt Anna is bringing pies." He glanced at Sara. "If Mom doesn't want to come, can I go with you, Sara?"

Sara met Mari's gaze. "I don't mean to put you on the spot. We all just think...you'd enjoy the experience."

Mari knew she shouldn't make the decision based on wanting to please her friends, or worse, to please James. Because at some point in the middle of the night, she realized she *did* want to please him. And that was dangerous. There couldn't be anything between her and James, and she needed to remember that. He was Amish and she wasn't, and even if that wasn't so, James didn't like her that way.

"Please, Mom? 'Kota won't be there. He goes to another church, but all the other guys will be there. J.J. says it's fun."

"Just to visit," Sara said softly. "To see how you feel about it."

"*Ya*, just come as a visitor," Ellie suggested as she tied her black bonnet over her *kapp*.

Mari watched Zachary dry his hands on a kitchen towel. "I can be ready in a minute, Mom. I promise I'll be good. Please?"

Mari smiled. How could she say no to her son when he was asking to go to church? And what harm would it do? It wasn't as if she had to decide on any lasting life changes today; like Sara said, she could go just to see how she felt about it.

So Mari went. And she sat on a bench with the other women, dressed in her long, navy blue skirt and scarf over her head, and she enjoyed the service far more than she anticipated.

When the final sermon and closing prayers of the service were finished, the younger men moved the benches and set up the tables for the communal meal. The women were equally busy removing food from baskets and containers and serving. As no work was done on the Sabbath, most of the meal was cold, but thanks to Johanna's advance planning, there were kettles of thick broth and vegetable soup simmering on the stoves. As Johanna and Roland's house was not a large one, the meal was served buffet-style, with tables reserved for the oldest and youngest members of the flock, while others stood to eat or balanced plates on their laps where they sat on the remaining chairs and benches.

Other than a warm smile or brief "We're so happy to have you with us today" from friends and neighbors, no one made much of Mari's presence among them. The feeling she received was one of total acceptance, and that was far easier than being pointed out for special notice and attention. She joined the other women in the kitchen, glad for something to keep her hands busy, and grateful for the satisfying routine of breaking bread together.

Twice Zachary passed through the kitchen. Once he and one of Anna's older boys were carrying a table in from the bench wagon used to carry furniture from house to house for worship. The second time, he'd come with Johanna's Jonah to find a mop to wipe up milk that a child had spilled. Both times, he'd grinned at her but hadn't lingered to talk.

Mari helped in the kitchen until everything seemed to be done that needing doing, and then she found her coat, put it on and stepped out onto the porch. She just needed a minute to be alone and take in the day's experience. Closing the door on the laughter and talk inside, she inhaled deeply of the frosty winter air. A light dusting of snow had transformed the stables and sheds and farmyard to a Grandma Moses painting, complete with a black-and-white cow sticking her head out a barn window and a flock of sheep gathered in the shelter of a covered well. Mari sank down on the back step, hugged herself and closed her eyes.

How long she sat there thinking of the bishop's touching sermon and listening to the echoes of the hymns in her mind she couldn't say, but gradually she realized that she was no longer alone.

"It means a lot to me that you came."

Mari's eyes snapped open. "James?" Immediately she felt silly. Who else could it be? She would know that deep and tender voice anywhere. "I'm sorry—you startled me," she said quickly, trying to cover her blunder. "I was daydreaming."

"Thinking about Bishop Atlee's sermon, I hope," he teased, taking a seat beside her on the step.

She glanced at him shyly. "Actually, I was. He's not a shouter, is he? Our bishop at home—where I grew up, I mean—he shook the rafters when he preached. Your Bishop Atlee speaks softly, and everyone gets quiet and leans forward to hear him. I like that."

"He's a good man. He has a good heart and a way to remind us of God's word without raising his voice. Preacher Reuben, Addy's father, now, *he* can get loud. And his sermons are a bit long, but…" James smiled and shrugged.

"Well, I do like your Bishop Atlee. He seems a wise man."

"One you might want to speak with. If you have questions," he added hastily. "Or you want to talk."

"It's good to know," she replied. It was nice here, sitting with James, her mind at ease, not worrying about anything, just enjoying the moment. "You're a good friend."

"Am I?" He smiled again in that lazy way, and his eyes gleamed with warmth and compassion.

"You are," she said. "I've only been here a week, but it feels like it's been months. Years."

She rested a hand on the step between them. The wood was cold and slightly damp, but the overhanging roof sheltered the steps. She didn't want the moment to end. Tomorrow would bring work, decisions to be made and a need to plan, moving out of Sara's house. But for now, she didn't have to worry about any of that. She could just sit there with James and enjoy the peace of the snowy afternoon.

James smiled at her, and they sat there for a little while in silence. Then he put his hands together. "I don't know about you, but I'm hungry. I think I'm going to try some of Johanna's vegetable soup. Can I interest you in joining me?"

"Sounds good." She rose to her feet, returning his smile. And suddenly she was hungry, not only for food but for the company of the others inside. For an instant her gaze met James's, and then she nodded and followed him into the warm kitchen.

He's my friend, she thought, and her heartbeat quickened. *My friend.* The sound of it was sweet, but a part of her wished... She shook her head, pushing the unthinkable away. *It's enough*, she thought. *It would be greedy to wish for more.*

Chapter Seven

The next morning, when Mari passed the plywood partition that closed off the addition from the rest of the house, she noticed a crude window cut through the plywood. She couldn't resist peering through and when she did, she spotted James, crouched on the floor. "Good morning," she said, pleasantly surprised to see him.

He looked up from the measurements he was taking on a board and smiled at her. "Good morning."

She didn't hear the now-familiar sounds of the men working. "Here all alone today?"

"Just passing through. I sent the crew to do a quick repair on a roof for the day." He stood up. "I came by because I wanted to tell you we won't be working today. I'm going with Mattie up to Wilmington, so I can't keep an eye on Zach. Hearing tests for the twins at A. I. du-Pont Children's Hospital."

"Oh, my. That sounds serious."

"Probably not. Just a precaution. Their pediatrician thinks the boys are probably fine, but he suggested the testing just to be sure."

"Your sister must be worried."

"*Ya*, but Mattie worries a lot." James approached the makeshift window. "I tried to tell her that there are enough things to worry about that you are certain of. It doesn't seem right to worry about possibilities. With Roman, she was worried about his speech. That little chipmunk didn't say a word until he was two. No *mam*, no *daddi*, not even *ne*. Mattie didn't think he'd ever talk."

Mari drew closer to James.

"*Ne*, not a word," James continued. "And then one morning Mattie made oatmeal for breakfast and Roman said, '*Ne*, want pancakes. Booberry.' Mattie was so tickled that she sent me to Byler's store to buy blueberries."

Mari chuckled. "So he started talking, just like that?"

James nodded. "Started jabbering and hasn't stopped yet. Talk your ears off. Emanuel was the opposite. He talked really young. Shouts most of the time. I think the twins are used to hearing the older two make so much racket, they don't pay attention to the little beeps and bells in the hearing test."

"Let's hope that's what it is," Mari said. She knew Zachary would be disappointed to hear that there wouldn't be any working going on in the addition today. That meant he'd have to stay with Sara while she was at work.

James picked up a hammer. "Why don't you stand back and I'll open this up. Once the last plywood is on the exterior, we'll have to start using this entrance."

She moved back several steps.

In less time than she would have expected, James took down two pieces of plywood, opening up an entrance-way that was the width of a double door. He stepped through with a flourish and a grin. "It won't be long now and Sara can start bringing in brides-to-be by the dozen."

"A dozen at a time? Goodness, that will be a full house!" Ellie came into the living room with three cups of coffee on a tray. As always, she was neat and pretty, blond hair peeking out from beneath her brilliant white *kapp* and blue eyes sparkling with energy. Ellie might have been a little person, but her personality was huge, and Mari liked her more every day.

"Big day," Ellie said, taking in the addition with a gesture. "It's actually starting to look like rooms." She offered Mari and James each a mug, indicating whose was whose. "Just the way you like it."

"Danki," James said. "Just what I need. I only got one cup this morning." He blew on the hot coffee and took a sip. "Where's Sara? She knew I planned on opening this doorway this morning. I thought she might want to see."

"She should be back soon. She had to make an early-morning phone call at the chair shop. Ruth's husband came to fetch her." She chuckled, looking at Mari. "A prospective client in Missouri with five unmarried daughters."

"Five?" James laughed. "Sara will find someone for every one of them. I don't know how she does it."

"Tell the truth, James," Ellie teased. "She's looking for someone special for you, too, isn't she? For all we know, Mattie could have hired Sara. I hear she's desperate to see you married within the year." Her eyes twinkled as she glanced at Mari. "Sara never tells a client's business unless they want it told."

Mari smiled at the two of them. She liked how comfortable they were with each other. James was definitely a different kind of Amish man than the taciturn uncle and male cousins with whom she'd grown up. Even the boys she'd known in school and the neighborhood had been much more formal with girls and women they weren't related to. She found James's kind, easy manner refreshing.

James motioned to them both. "Come on in. Take a look. There's going to be a bedroom, a full bathroom and a big parlor downstairs, and three big bedrooms and another full bathroom upstairs. Plus some closets. Now that we have heat from the woodstove, the inside finishing will come together fast."

"I love all the windows," Mari said. "And the oak staircase will be lovely." Although the Sheetrock hadn't gone up yet, she could imagine what the space would look like once it was done. The wood-burning stove was a high-efficiency model made of soapstone from Sweden that was popular in Wisconsin and gave off a steady heat.

"I feel bad that I didn't let you know about not being able to keep an eye on Zach," James said to Mari. "There was a cancellation." He set down his coffee cup and picked up a broom. "The doctor's office left a message Friday on the chair shop's answering machine, but Mattie didn't get it until last night." He began to sweep. "Any progress on getting Zachary in school?"

She sighed. "The new school won't take him until they have his records, so that's what we're waiting on."

James swept the sawdust into a pile. "How long will that take?"

"I'm not sure. Honestly, it's my fault. It never occurred to me that they wouldn't take him without them," Mari said. She set down her coffee mug, picked up the dustpan and stooped to hold it for him.

"I'm sorry I can't spend time with Zach today."

"Oh, don't be silly. He'll be fine here with Sara." She glanced up at him. "Although I'm sure he'd rather spend the day working with you. Sara's liable to put him to work folding laundry or dusting furniture."

"Why don't I take him to school with me?" Ellie offered, sipping her coffee.

"I don't know," Mari said slowly.

"Can't I just go with James? I don't want to go to the Amish school."

Mari turned to see Zachary standing in the new door opening to the living room. He was wearing jeans and his pajama top. "Please don't be rude to Ellie," she said quietly. It hadn't been so much what he said as how he said it.

"Or to your mother," James said quietly.

Zachary's features lost their defiant expression, and he looked down at his feet. "Sorry," he mumbled. He looked up again. "But I don't want to go to school. I want to build stuff. Like James."

Mari emptied the dustpan into a bucket of trash. She rested the dustpan against the wall and went to her son. "Not going to school was never an option, Zachary. You know that."

He set his jaw. "It's not fair."

Ellie glanced at Mari, then at Zachary. "What I was wondering, Zach, was if you'd be willing to come give me a hand today at school? Not as a student. More of a helper."

Interest sparked in Zachary's eyes, but he averted his gaze. "Will I get paid?"

"Zachary!" Mari's eyes widened. "You don't ask people for money."

"I'll not give you a penny," Ellie said with a smile,

not in the least bit fazed. "Just a big thank-you from me. James has been telling me what a help you are to his crew, and I thought I could borrow you for the day."

Zachary rubbed one stockinged foot against the other. "I don't know…"

Mari turned to James. Ellie's offer sounded like a great idea to her, but Zachary, realizing how she felt, might work against her. "What do you think, James? You think Zachary would be any help to Ellie at school?"

He nodded. "I do. He can be a big help, when he wants to be." He looked to Zachary. "I have to leave in a minute, but I could actually use your help right now moving a piece of plywood." He hooked his thumb in the direction of the far end of the addition. "You have time?"

Zachary looked to his mother, and she nodded. "Be right back," he said and ran after James.

Mari watched as Zachary followed James. Her son, she noticed, had thrust his hands into his pockets just as James had. "He has the magic touch, doesn't he?" she said to Ellie, watching them. "Zachary has taken to him. I'm constantly hearing 'James says this' or 'James does that.'"

"He's a good role model," Ellie agreed. "None better. He'll make a fine husband and a fine father."

Mari looked at her, suddenly wondering if she'd been so caught up in her own life that she'd missed something going on between Ellie and James. "Wait…" She pointed to James and then Ellie. "You and James, you're not—"

"Oh, no." Ellie laughed. "We're friends." Her smile was so wide that her dimples showed. "Good friends but just friends. We wouldn't be suited. I'm in no hurry to be wed, and I've made that clear to Sara. I'm a schoolteacher. It's a job I've wanted since I was six years old. If I marry, I have to give up the school, and I have no intention of doing that anytime soon."

Mari picked up her mug and took a sip of her coffee. "But all Amish women marry. At least most of them do. Don't you want a husband, a family?"

Ellie's features creased into a smile over the rim of her mug. "Sure I do. Someday but not yet. I'll teach a while first, get it out of my system. Then I'll let Sara find me a good man with broad shoulders and a gentle heart." She looked up at Mari. "How about you?"

"Me?"

"Would you like to be married?" Ellie asked.

Mari felt far more comfortable talking about Ellie's future than her own. "I...I don't know," she answered honestly. "I've been so busy trying to put a roof over our heads that I haven't thought much about it, I guess." She sighed. "I think I would like to be married again. To have a husband, but...I'm not sure I trust myself to choose a man I'd want to spend the rest of my life with." She pressed her lips together. "I made a pretty poor choice once."

Ellie caught Mari's hand and gave it a squeeze before letting it go. "That's why you let family or friends help you choose. Or a matchmaker." Her tone turned teasing. "Sara would make the perfect match for you—I know she would."

"You mean an Amish match?"

Ellie lifted one shoulder and let it fall. "If that's what you decide you want."

Mari found herself gazing off in the direction James had gone with Zachary, her hands wrapped around the still-warm coffee mug. "The thing is, I don't know what I want," she said softly.

"That's okay," Ellie assured her. "You don't have to know all the answers all the time. Sometimes we just need to sit back and see what God has planned for us. And *relax*."

Mari thought about the previous day, about church and how good it had felt to be there. And how she had felt a nearness to God that she hadn't felt in a very long time. So maybe Ellie was right. Maybe she did just need to relax and see what He had in store for her.

Ellie glanced down at the watch she wore attached to her apron. "*Ach.* Look at the time. I'd better get my lunch packed. And I think I'll pack one for Zachary, too. Just in case he decides to take me up on my offer."

"You don't have to do this," Mari said, on steadier ground talking about Zachary than herself.

"I want to. And he really would be a help. I know you probably don't always see it, but your Zachary is a very sweet boy."

"Who's sweet?" Zachary asked, coming toward them.

Ellie put a hand on her hip. She might have been barely as tall as Zachary, but she appeared imposing just the same. "Are you coming with me or not?"

"Yeah, I'll come," he agreed.

"*Goot.* Now, if you want anything besides egg-salad sandwiches, you'd best come give me a hand packing our lunches."

Zachary glanced at Mari and she nodded. "Go. Have a good day. And make sure you don't cause trouble. And thank you, Ellie," she called after her. "You're a lifesaver."

"Don't worry about the boy," James said quietly

when Ellie and Zachary disappeared into the kitchen. "Ellie's tough. She won't let him get away with anything."

Mari sighed. "Sometimes, I don't think I'm tough enough. And other times I'm convinced that I expect too much of him." She offered James a grateful look. "I don't know what you said to convince him to go with Ellie, but thank you."

"No problem. He reminds me a lot of myself at that age."

She stood there for a minute in comfortable silence with James, then picked up his empty coffee mug to take it to the kitchen with her own. "Well, if you'll excuse me, I've got to eat something before I go to work. I hope everything goes well today. Safe travels."

"Mari?" he called after her as she turned away.

She turned back.

"I almost forgot," James said. "Mattie wanted you and Zach to come to supper tomorrow night."

"At your house?" She hesitated, wondering if she should. When she'd come to Seven Poplars, she thought it would be just a place to stop over on her way to a better life for her and Zachary. She hadn't expected to become so...*involved* in everyone's lives. She hadn't expected to make so many friends. And she couldn't help wondering if it was a mistake. If it would just make it harder when she left.

"Please come. I'll be happy to ride over and get you. It would be a big favor to me. Lilly's coming and bringing her cousin. Mattie is determined to throw Lilly and me together. And with her cousin, I'm afraid I'll be outnumbered, three to one. I need a friend to back me up."

Mari chuckled. "Well, when you put it that way." She

gave a nod. "I'll be happy to have dinner with your family. I've been wanting to get to know your sister and the rest of your nephews." She liked the idea of him needing a favor from her. It was what friends did, wasn't it?

"Just be prepared for anything," he said with a grin. "And *never*, ever turn your back on Emanuel. The last time Bishop Atlee came to supper, he put a cricket in his soup."

As it turned out, Zachary didn't go with her to James's house for supper. Hannah Yoder was having some of her grandchildren over for an evening of homemade soup, corn muffins and apple pie. Zachary had explained after coming home his second day at the Amish school that they would make popcorn balls and hot cocoa the old-fashioned way at Hannah's and he didn't want to miss it. 'Kota, J.J. and Jonah would be there as well as a few boys from school. Anna's twins, who were older, were coming over to walk with him to Hannah's house and see him safely back to Sara's. Mari tried to explain to Zachary that he was expected to dinner at James's sister's house, but he couldn't be swayed. He really wanted to be with the other boys.

What could she do? She let him go.

"Don't worry about him," James said after she climbed into his buggy and explained why Zachary wasn't accepting Mattie's invitation. "Hannah will keep an eye on him. He won't get into any trouble on her watch. You want him to make friends, don't you?"

"I'm just amazed, I guess," she confessed. "In the community where I grew up, we never played with English kids. And we certainly didn't have English kids at school with us. Having worldly friends wasn't encouraged."

James snapped the leathers over his horse's back. "Walk on," he said to Jericho. And then to her, "But Zachary is a special case, isn't he? You were raised in the faith. According to our tradition, that makes your boy one of us, whether he likes it or not. In our eyes, he's no different than the other children in our community, because none of the children are baptized."

Neither of them said anything after that, and for a few minutes there was only the comforting rhythm of Jericho's ironclad hooves striking the blacktop. A few snowflakes were drifting down like confetti. The air was crisp and cold, and the quiet of the countryside surrounded them like a velvet cloak. It seemed nice to Mari to just be able to ride in silence with James. There was something comforting about their quiet companionship, something she didn't quite understand.

"So how did the twins' appointment go?" Mari asked.

"Great." He grinned. "The boys are fine. Hearing is fine. No need to see the specialist again."

"That must be a relief," she said. Then, after a few minutes, "I was thinking this morning. Do you know that no one here has asked me about Zachary's father?"

"They won't." He uttered a muffled grunt of amusement. "Well, Addy's mother, Martha, might, but no one would expect you to answer her." He cut his eyes at her. "Has anyone warned you about Martha?"

"Sort of. Gideon said if she came into the shop, let her have anything she wanted, free of charge. And not to do anything to ruffle her feathers."

"Smart man, Gideon. It's why he gets on so well with his in-laws. So long as Martha does nothing to upset Addy or cause trouble between him and his wife, Gideon lets Martha have her druthers."

"So Martha's something of a character, is she?"

She could see him grinning in the darkness. "You could say that. Gideon once told me that he suspects she eats unripe persimmons. Otherwise, she couldn't come up with all the sour things she has to say about her relatives and neighbors. But he says she has a good heart—she just doesn't realize that some of the things she says can be hurtful."

"It's hard for me to believe that there's not more than a little whispering going on about me. I'm a woman alone with a son. I know Amish. They're as human as anyone else, and, religious or not, they like to gossip."

"Some do," he admitted. "But we've all made mistakes. And Sara likes you. Gideon and Addy praise your work. And anyone who disagreed with them would have to face down Ellie. She's quite an ally."

"She is, isn't she?" Mari smiled at the thought. Ellie was probably one of the best friends she'd ever had. It seemed to have happened overnight. And so easily. She glanced at James. "What about you? Have you wondered about Zachary's father?"

James shrugged. "None of my business. I figured if you want me to know, you'll tell me. I gather he's not really part of Zachary's life."

"No. He died." She let out a long breath, realizing that it felt good to confide in James. She waited for the old hurt to twist in the pit of her stomach, but all she felt was a twinge of sadness and regret for Ivan's passing. "He was Amish," she said. "We made a mistake and we ran away together, but he wasn't prepared for the outside world. He had a harder time adjusting than

I did, maybe because he'd been baptized and he knew there was no going back."

"Mari, it's okay," James said quietly. "There's no need for you to share this with me."

She swallowed. "I don't mind. I...I'd like to tell you." He didn't say anything, just waited patiently, so she went on, "We were both young. I thought I was in love. Things just went too fast. We made some impulsive decisions. Then we had a new life to be responsible for. That was too much for Ivan. He turned wild. Fell in with the wrong crowd and did things I couldn't accept."

"He ran out on you."

She shook her head. "Not with other girls. He wasn't like that. He had a good heart in spite of his immaturity. But the things he was doing, the people he brought to our place? I didn't want them around our child."

"So you took on the full responsibility for yourself and your baby?"

"He left when I was seven months along. I tried to contact him when Zachary was born, but I think he was in jail. I never saw him again." She closed her eyes. "It was Sara who wrote to me and told me about the accident. Zachary was about four. Ivan and another ex-Amish boy were killed in a car accident. Ivan was driving."

James turned the horse off the road and onto his lane. "I'm so sorry, Mari. It must have been terrible for you."

"Terrible that I was so stupid, that I'd allowed such a thing to happen, that I'd left everything I knew and cared for behind. If Ivan and I had stayed, made confession and been forgiven, I'm afraid it would have been worse. I would have been married to a foolish boy who thought more about a good time than the fact that he was going to be a father."

"You told me that you went back to your uncle's that one time. Did you ever think about trying it again? Maybe going to some other member of the community?"

"I did." She sighed. "A couple of times...maybe a lot of times. But I was stubborn and proud. And I could never have stood in the church and said I had sinned and regretted what I'd done. My son isn't a mistake. He's good and pure and the most decent thing in my life."

"The faith can be hard to live by, but we really do believe in forgiveness. In God's mercy. In His love. I don't think anyone could expect you to deny your son's worth."

"My uncle did. He said the only way I could come back was to send him away, to let him be adopted by a married couple. Somewhere far away, where I'd never see him again. I couldn't do it. I *wouldn't* do it. So my aunt and uncle crossed my name out of the family Bible and said I was dead to them." Lights from the house grew larger as the horse approached it. She cleared her throat. "I'm sorry. I shouldn't have brought all of this up." She stared out at the gorgeous snowflakes, feeling a strange comfort in the sound of Jericho's hoofbeats. "I'm not much of a supper guest, am I?"

"We're friends, Mari, and this is what friends are for, right?" He reached over and patted her hand. "I'm honored that you'd share with me."

His hand felt good, the warmth, the security of it. But she also took note of the fact that he used the term *friends*. "I just hope we'll still be friends, now that you know what a wicked woman I am."

He laughed and took his hand from hers. "Hardly

wicked. And don't worry. I don't discuss my friends' personal matters with other people, not even with my sister." He stopped the buggy at the front of the house. The door opened, and a man and woman stepped out. "There she is. Mattie," he said. "And her husband, Rupert. He surprised us by showing up this afternoon. You go in and get warm. I'm going to put Jericho in the barn."

Mari climbed down, and Mattie rushed out to meet her. "Come in—come in," she said cheerfully.

"Welcome." Rupert said.

"Everyone else is here," Mattie bubbled. "Lilly and her cousin can't wait to meet you. And the children are so excited that their *fadder* is home, they're worse than usual."

In minutes, Mari was inside and Rupert had taken her coat. Mattie, a smaller, rounder, ditzy version of James, had led her through the front room and into the kitchen and shown her to a chair at the round table. Scooping up a crying baby, she deposited him into Mari's arms and introduced Lilly Hershberger and her cousin Calvin, also a Hershberger. When James said Lilly was bringing her cousin, Mari had assumed he meant another girl. Calvin was a very tall, very slim man with yellow-blond hair.

Little William in Mari's arms was crying so loudly that she could barely hear what Lilly said to her. Trying to settle him, she rested him on her shoulder and bounced him. It felt surprisingly good to have a baby in her arms again.

"Wait," Mattie said laughing. "Let me trade you. You hold Timothy here. He never cries." She took a swaddled infant from Lilly and looked down into his face.

"Or is this William?" A puzzled expression came over her face. "Lilly, did I tell you this one was Timothy?"

Lilly, who Mari had met at church Sunday, was a very pretty young woman with dimples on each cheek and curly blond hair much lighter than Ellie's. She laughed. "You said you thought he was Timothy, but you weren't sure."

Mattie met her husband's gaze.

"Don't look at me." Rupert grinned, holding up both hands. "You know I can't tell the twins apart except when you tie ribbons on their wrists."

James came in through the kitchen door just then.

"Sit there," Mattie instructed. "Next to Lilly." She handed him the baby she'd taken from Lilly. "We're not sure which one he is," she told James. "I'm going to start putting the food on the table."

"Can I help?" Lilly asked Mattie, while smiling at James.

"*Ne, ne*, you sit," Mattie said. The toddler Emanuel crawled out from under the table and seized a hold of his mother's skirts. "Emanuel. Up on your stool beside your *fadder*. Rupert, can you get him? Where did Roman get to? Roman? Come to the table." She rushed to the stove and began dishing up bowls of vegetables.

The baby that James was holding opened his eyes and began to whimper. James put him up on his shoulder and began patting the little boy on his back. The baby gave a loud burp.

Everyone laughed.

"I can see you're an old hand at that," Lilly said, clearly smitten with James. "You'll make some woman a *goot* husband."

Rupert took the now-sleeping baby from Mari's arms

and laid him in a cradle near the stove and came back to retrieve the second twin from James and snuggle him in with his brother. Then Rupert put Roman on a stool beside James and went to help his wife bring the food to the table.

"Wait until you hear our news, James," Rupert said after he and Mattie had taken their seats and they had shared grace. "My mother has agreed to come live with us." He took two slices of ham and passed the platter to Calvin. "She'll be selling her house and helping us with the cost of putting up our cabin. Which means," he said, exchanging meaningful glances with his wife, "that you'll have your home to yourself much sooner than you expected."

Mari met James's gaze across the table. *See what I'm talking about*, he seemed to be saying. She had to look away to keep from laughing out loud.

Chapter Eight

For a second, James didn't respond to Rupert's obvious hint that once he and Mattie and the boys were gone, James would be free to bring home a wife. From across the table, he could see that Mari was trying not to laugh, her pretty eyes dancing. He almost started laughing himself, though he didn't know why. This wasn't a laughing matter. He really *was* going to have to sit Mattie down and have a talk with her. No underhanded or heavy-handed matchmaking his sister could do was going to sway him. He thought he'd made that clear to her. He wasn't going to marry Lilly Hershberger or any other girl just to make Mattie happy.

James grinned. "I'm in no hurry to be rid of you," he told Rupert as he threw out his hand to catch a glass of milk that Roman had just tipped over. James wasn't fast enough, but fortunately the three-year-old had already drunk most of the milk. James laid his napkin on the puddle as his sister leaped to her feet. "It's fine," he said. "I've got it."

"*Ne*, let me." Lilly offered James her napkin. "Cleaning up after children is women's work."

Calvin nodded. "Let her do it, James. It's always been that way in our family. Plenty of men's work outside, *ya*?"

"I'd say the wisest thing is that the job should go to whoever's closest," James replied. "And the one that will end up with milk in his lap if he doesn't jump fast." He chuckled, and the others joined in.

"I'm sorry," Roman murmured in *Deitsch*.

"No harm done," James assured his nephew as he eased back into his chair and reached for a bowl of green beans in front of him.

Calvin picked up a serving bowl and held it out to Mari. "Scalloped potatoes?"

"Thanks," Mari said.

Calvin took a generous helping for himself before passing the dish on to her.

As the evening meal progressed, it didn't escape James's notice that Lilly's cousin Calvin had been admiring Mari since they'd arrived. She had dressed modestly in a dark navy dress that he'd seen her wear before. She had pinned her hair up into a bun at the back of her neck, but she wore no head covering. Not that she should. It was only required for Amish, traditional Mennonites and other religious groups, not the English. But she was wearing nothing revealing, nothing that would not pass a deacon's scrutiny. She had dark stockings or tights on over her legs and sensible black sneakers. There was no reason for Calvin to keep staring at her, unless he found her attractive.

Not only had Calvin paid more attention to Mari than he should, he'd done a lot of talking to her about his plans to raise ducks commercially and for buying a farm in the area. He'd rambled on at length about the modern house he was looking for, emphasizing that he'd been single long enough and had reached an age to settle down and find a wife.

James glanced at Mari; he hoped she was having a good time. She seemed to like Mattie, and Mattie obviously liked her. If she didn't, James would have known. His sister was a force to be reckoned with and a woman who liked to have things her way, but in spite of all that he would truly miss her family when they moved into their own house. He loved Mattie and the children dearly, and he was very fond of his brother-in-law. But Mattie never let go of a notion once it had settled over her, and she always had *some* notion.

James took a bite of scalloped potatoes. Calvin was still talking about ducks. It was a shame that he and Lilly were related, because *they* would have suited each other. Calvin and Lilly both liked to talk about themselves best.

Calvin seemed nice enough, but it was obvious that he wasn't right for Mari. James seriously doubted that Calvin would understand the responsibility that came with taking a wife who had a nine-year-old son. The wrong husband and stepfather, and life would be unhappy for all three of them.

Rupert, probably tired of hearing about ducks, cleared his throat as Calvin took a breath and spoke quickly to get in before Calvin got wound up again. "How's the addition at Sara Yoder's going, James?"

"Well." He nodded, wishing he'd gotten up to get a clean napkin. He hoped he didn't have any potato in the corner of his mouth. He tried to wipe at it inconspicuously. "I opened the new rooms to the main house this morning."

"James is a wonderful carpenter." Lilly beamed at James. "He does beautiful work. Everyone says so."

"He's promised to build the cabinets for our new house," Rupert said. Emanuel chose that moment to slide from his stool to try to dive under the table. His father caught him by the back of the shirt collar and helped him firmly, but gently, back into his seat. "Sit still, son," he warned, "or no pie for you."

"Lilly brought two cherry pies for dessert," Mattie said. "Her cherry pie raised twenty-two dollars at the last school fund-raising."

Unfair, James thought. Mattie knew cherry was his favorite pie. He never could resist it, and he suspected that his sister had put Lilly up to baking it. He should have been pleased, but he felt like a shoat that was being funneled down a ramp into the slaughter room at the back of the butcher shop. Next Mattie would be talking about spring weddings.

"Muscovy or Runners. Both good layers," Calvin announced to the table and then moved on to the subject of different breeds of ducks and the possibility of finding a market for duck eggs.

James could see that Mari was trying to pay attention, but her eyes were beginning to glaze over. *So much for the duck farmer*, James thought. *He's duck soup.*

Eventually, Mattie took pity on them all and asked Mari about the different style of the women's prayer *kapps* in Wisconsin, and Mari gratefully gave her a detailed description of the head covering. Calvin, undeterred by his hostess's attempt to change the subject, asked Mari if she'd ever baked with duck eggs. When she admitted she hadn't but had seen her aunt use them in custards, Calvin seized the topic and explained why the larger duck egg was superior to a chicken's in bread pudding.

Somehow they made it through the supper, one twin's wailing, the cherry pies and a lopsided German chocolate cake that Mattie had baked, and Roman and Emanuel's protests at being sent to bed. The rest of the evening went fairly well, and James was just beginning to think about suggesting he hitch up Jericho to take Mari home. He'd had such a good time riding over with her that he'd been looking forward to the ride home all evening. Then Calvin beat him to it and offered to drive her home.

"We're going right past Sara's house," Calvin explained. "It would be foolish for James to go out when there's plenty of room in our buggy."

"It's not a problem," James said.

"Ne," Lilly chimed in. "James has to be hard at work at Sara's early tomorrow morning. We're glad to see her home. I insist."

A few minutes later, James followed Mari and the others out the door, amid a flurry of thank-yous and "You must come again soon," and helped her into the back of Lilly's father's family buggy.

"I hope you enjoyed yourself," James said to Mari as he found the lap robe under the seat and handed it to her. "I warned you that it would be chaotic."

"I had a great time." She smiled down at him. "The children are adorable."

"Even Emanuel?"

She chuckled. "Especially Emanuel."

James wanted to say something about the fact that he was sorry he wasn't going to get to drive her home, but he didn't know how to say it, so he just said good-bye. "I guess I'll see you tomorrow."

She smiled at him again, and James wished the evening wasn't over.

James returned to the kitchen to find Mattie settled down in her rocker near the stove, feeding the babies. He grabbed a clean dishcloth and started wiping off the table.

"So, James," Rupert said, a broom in hand. "Are you planning on asking Lilly to walk out with you?"

Mattie sighed. "Men." She rolled her eyes. "Not a clue. Didn't you see them together?" she asked her husband, though not unkindly. "I had high hopes, but James is as flighty as a yearling steer in fly season. He's not interested in courting Lilly."

Rupert paused to look at James. "I thought you were tired of the bachelor life."

"Lilly would make any man a fine wife." James leaned on the table to look back at his brother-in-law. "I like her, but that's not enough to make me choose her as my partner for life."

Mattie sniffed. "It's Mari Troyer who's caught his eye."

James glanced at her.

"Don't give me that innocent look of yours," she cautioned. "I saw the looks you two were giving each other across the table...*and* the dirty looks you were giving Calvin."

"I don't know what you're talking about." James wiped down the chair Roman had been sitting in, catching the crumbs with his hand. "But someone needs to tell that boy that there's only so much duck information a person can handle in one sitting."

"Don't try to skitter away from the subject," Mattie warned. "You like Sara's Mari."

"Of course I like her." James carried his handful of crumbs to the trashcan. "She's my friend."

"Just a friend?" Mattie asked. "The way you were watching her all evening? I'm afraid that it's more than just friendship there, brother."

"Oooh, getting warm in here." Rupert propped his broom against the wall. "Let me have those babies, Mattie, if they're asleep. I'll just carry them upstairs and tuck them into their cribs." Gathering up both babies, he gave James a glad-it's-not-me-in-hot-water look and made himself scarce.

"Don't you like her, Mattie?" James said quietly after his brother-in-law had left the room. "It seemed to me as if you two got on fine tonight."

Mattie rose and went to him, placing both hands on his shoulders. "Of course I like her. She's a good person. But you seem to be forgetting that Mari's not Amish. She walked away from the church."

"So did I, but I came back." He studied her face; she had their mother's eyes. "You saw Mari in church this week. Sara thinks she'll return to the faith. And so do I."

Mattie squeezed his arm. "You know how much I've always loved you and wanted what was best for you."

"I do." His voice came out thick and full of emotion. He loved Mattie, too, deeply, and he never wanted to hurt her. But sometimes they didn't see eye to eye, and he refused to give in to her just because he loved her. "And I gave you my word that I was back for good. I won't marry outside the church. You don't need to worry about that."

"How can I not worry?"

"I'm not the little brother who needs you to care for his skinned knees anymore. I'm a grown man, and I can take care of myself."

"It's not your knees I'm worried about. I'm afraid you're going to get your heart broken." She gazed up at him, her eyes teary in the lamplight. "Even if Mari does come back and accept baptism, how will you know that she won't leave again? Leave and take your children with her? Then you'd have to go, wouldn't you?"

"You have to trust me, Mattie. I know you mean well, but I'll pick my own wife when I'm good and ready."

"But not an Englisher. Promise me that," she begged. "And promise me that you'll think about what you're doing with Mari, the risk you're taking. You know, when I started to come of courting age, our *dat* warned me never to walk out with a man I wouldn't marry. I think it was wise advice."

"I'm not walking out with Mari. Mattie, you're the one who told me to invite her to supper. Tonight was just a supper with friends."

She gave him a look that made it clear she wasn't buying it. "Promise me," she repeated.

He exhaled. "I promise you I'll always take into consideration what you have to say. I value your advice, but in the end, the decision is mine. And you can rest your mind on one thing. I'd never consider an English girl."

"Have it your way," she said, releasing him and retracing her steps to the rocking chair. "Stay friends with Mari. And I'm not saying there's anything wrong with that. But find yourself a good Amish girl, someone who's never strayed from the fold, someone who will help you put down roots in this community. Marriage isn't just between a man and a woman. When you make your wedding vows, you marry a family, a community, and you make a commitment to your future children and grandchildren." Her gaze locked with his, and he felt the strength of her conviction. "Mari Troyer is a good woman and a good mother, but I don't want her as a sister-in-law. You think about that, James. And if you're wise, you won't let this *friendship* of yours go any deeper."

When business picked up late in the afternoon at the butcher shop, Mari left her desk in the office and went out to help wait on customers. She didn't mind the change of pace. She'd been working on orders and taking phone calls all day. Wrapping meat and ringing up sales was easy. She was just checking out a nice English woman with a toddler when she spotted James coming through the front door. Just catching sight of him made her smile. "Hi," she called to him. She handed the customer her receipt and her bag. "Thanks, come again," she told the customer.

James waited for the woman to walk away and then came to the counter. "I'd like four center-cut pork chops and two pounds of bacon, please," he said. "Mattie wants thick, lean chops."

"Sure." He was grinning, though why she didn't know. She couldn't help but grin back. "I'll be happy to get that for you. How was your day?" she asked as she pulled on clear plastic gloves and opened the meat display.

"Good. Good." He nodded. "Sara's addition is coming along. We'll be done before you know it. How about you?" He watched her place the chops on a piece of butcher paper on the scale. "Good day?"

"Great." And having him pop in like this made it better, but she didn't say that, of course.

He glanced at the big clock on the wall. "Don't you usually leave around this time?"

"About this time," she told him as she wrapped up his chops.

He nodded and slid his hands into his pockets. "Business good?"

"Picking up every day," she answered.

"Seems like you've settled in fast. Thomas mentioned to me that Gideon told him you were a great worker." He picked up a box of crackers from beside the register, looked at them and put them back. "I was wondering if you'd like a ride home to Sara's."

She looked up from the register at him in surprise. "That's nice of you to offer. I was going to take the van. They leave in half an hour." She gave him the total of his purchase.

James slid bills across the counter. "I know you can ride home with them, but I'm saying you should ride home with me. I have to stop at Byler's store, for Mattie. And Sara wants half-and-half for something, so I have to go by there on the way home anyway." He reached for the pork chops. "I figured you might like to go. You said you were getting your first paycheck."

"I don't know." She chewed on her lower lip. "Zachary might wonder where I am if I'm late," she said, although she really did want to go. To pick up a few things, of course. Not just so she could ride home with James.

"Funny you should say that because Sara said to remind you that Zachary and Ellie would be late this afternoon. Something about an errand at Johanna and Roland's. So you don't need to worry about him."

"You told Sara you were picking me up?" she asked.

"I told her I was going to ask you."

Mari stood there, not sure what to do. She did want to buy deodorant and shampoo, and this would be the perfect opportunity. If she went with James now, she wouldn't have to try to catch a ride into town with someone in their neighborhood tomorrow.

Byler's was a Mennonite country store that had started out as a discount grocery and had grown to include kitchen goods, fruits and vegetables, frozen food and cold cuts. It was as large as many English chain groceries, and the prices were reasonable. Best of all, it was only two miles from the butcher shop.

James tucked the packet of chops under his arm. "Come on. You know you want to go. What's wrong with taking a ride from a friend?"

"Nothing, I suppose. Not a thing wrong with it," she said when she met his reassuring gaze. "But I have something I have to finish in the office. Can you wait ten minutes?"

He smiled. "And not five minutes longer."

She grimaced as she pulled off her apron and hurried toward the back to close out the last order of the day. "You've found my weakness," she called over her shoulder. "I tend to run late."

"Not for Byler's tonight, we don't. You run late and you'll miss your chance for me to buy you one of the best ice-cream cones in the county. They close at six o'clock in the winter, and it will be mobbed the last half hour."

They arrived at the store a little after five o'clock,

and it was packed. The English shoppers, mostly senior citizens, outnumbered the Amish three to one, but she saw plenty of Mennonite and Amish families shopping. There was even a young Amish father shopping alone with an adorable little pigtailed girl in his cart and a four-year-old boy walking beside him. The girl wore a blue dress, black stockings and black boots, and a tight-fitting white baby *kapp*, while the boy was an exact copy of his father. Mari couldn't resist, and she waved and said hi in *Deitsch*. Shyly, the small boy hid his face in his father's pant leg, but his sister smiled and waved back.

James gave her a quick tour of the store; then they went their separate ways so he could pick up the spices and the raw sugar Mattie had requested. Mari grabbed what she needed and met him at the registers. By the time she got there, he had just paid for his items.

"I'll run these out and get our ice-cream cones—before they close," he told her.

"It's all right—we don't need ice cream. We'll spoil our supper," she teased, pushing her little cart forward in the checkout line.

"Never. It's like an appetizer," he insisted, tugging the brim of his black hat down. "And I already paid for them. Meet you right here in a couple of minutes." He backed away from her toward the door. "What flavor would you like?"

"Surprise me," she replied and shook her head, laughing as he hurried out the door.

A short time later James met her at the front of the store with two huge ice-cream cones. "That's more ice cream than we can possibly eat," she told him, unable to stop smiling.

"Bet it's not. Chocolate mint chip or butter pecan?" He held out the cones for her to choose.

It took her a second to decide because she loved both. "Chocolate mint chip," she declared.

He handed her the cone. "Want me to take your bag?"

"No, I'm fine." She found the ice cream to be every bit as creamy and delicious as he had described it on the way over.

"We can sit at one of those picnic tables," he told her, leading the way to a small eating area that was set up at the front of the store.

"That's fine." She followed him.

"And then we'll head home."

"Thank you," she said between bites when they were seated across from each other at one of the tables. "This is delicious." She was so glad that she'd come. Being with James was fun, and she found him so easy to talk to. She felt as if she could be herself with him. He made her comfortable with who she was, the good and the bad. "Be certain to tell Mattie how much I enjoyed her meal," she reminded him.

"I will. You know, she really likes you," he said. Then it seemed as if he wanted to say something more.

She took another lick of her cone and reached for the napkin holder in the center of the table. "But?"

He exhaled. "I probably shouldn't even say this but... I feel like we can tell each other anything. I mean, I know we haven't known each other long, but—"

"But I get you. And you get me," she dared, not knowing what made her so bold to say such a thing. After all, they really *hadn't* known each other long. And what's more, their friendship wasn't typical. Amish men weren't usually friends with English women. They didn't shop or sit down to eat ice cream together. She passed him one of the napkins. "Tell me what Mattie said."

He exhaled. "She's worried that you could be a bad influence on me. Actually, I think she's worried that we'll be a bad influence on each other."

Mari frowned. "How?"

"I don't know. I'm not saying it makes sense. It's just what she said. She thinks that my being friends with you will make me want to return to the English world."

Mari thought for a moment before responding. It was upsetting to think that Mattie was concerned about her friendship with James, but she was glad he had told her. She could tell that it had been weighing on his mind. "Do I make you wish you were English again?"

He gave her a little smirk that made him look younger than he was. "Not hardly. I've had my fill of pickup trucks and wide-screen TVs. I belong in these clothes." He indicated his hat and denim coat. "Driving that buggy." He pointed to Jericho waiting patiently in the parking lot.

"James, I don't want to cause trouble between you and your sister," she said. "And it's certainly not my intention to convince anyone to leave Seven Poplars. I mean, I'm the one who came here from the big, bad world, and I have to admit, the change has been really nice. I like my life at Sara's and I like Seven Poplars." Certainly better than the life she'd had in Wisconsin.

"I told Mattie that."

She thought again for a minute. She was down to the crunchy cone now. "You said she thought we were a bad influence on each other, but you're definitely not a bad influence on me." She hesitated. "You know, I think I went to church Sunday mostly because *you* wanted me to." She smiled. "But I'm so glad I did."

"I'm glad you came, too. Now, I don't want you to turn into a worrier. I told my sister that I choose my own friends and I meant it."

Mari picked up her napkins and wiped her mouth, trying to ignore the small twinge of disappointment. James had used that word again. *Friend.*

"James?" A tall, angular woman in a black dress and bonnet walked out of the checkout area. "I'm surprised to see you here at this time of the day. Cut out early, didn't you?" She was speaking to James but staring at Mari.

Mari recognized her as Gideon's mother-in-law, Martha.

"And Mari Troyer. I'm surprised to see you here." Her voice was as grating as fingernails across a blackboard. "Is Sara with you?"

Mari could tell by the woman's tone of voice that she knew very well that Sara wasn't with them. "She's not," Mari managed.

"Ellie?" Martha demanded.

James shook his head, finishing up his ice-cream cone and wiping his mouth with one of the napkins Mari had given him. "Afraid not."

Martha pursed her lips. "So you're here together? Unchaperoned?"

James chuckled. "Guilty, Martha."

Martha frowned, unfazed by James's charm. "You haven't been in Seven Poplars long, Mari," she said, turning to her again. "Not long at all. And I don't know what kind of rules you had in Wisconsin. But here, it's best if a young woman doesn't give others a reason to question her behavior." She glanced back at James. "Unless the two of you are courting and I haven't heard?"

She raised her eyebrows at James, and Mari was surprised when he didn't answer.

"Well," Martha huffed. Then she cleared her throat. "You know, Mari, some may think I'm a gossip, but I'm not. I'm just a woman who likes to speak her mind. So I'm coming right out and asking." She looked at James again. "Are you two walking out together?"

James got to his feet. "We're just buying groceries, Martha. I was coming to Byler's, and Mari needed a ride. The most scandalous thing we've done is eat ice cream before supper. But thank you for your concern." He balled up his napkin and tossed it in a trash can.

Martha drew herself up to her full height, and her eyes narrowed. "No need to get snippy with me, young man. I'm simply trying to point out to Mari that it's easy for a girl to be talked about. And Seven Poplars is not Hollywood."

Not sure what to say, Mari said nothing. She didn't want to get James in trouble. Martha held up her hand as if making a proclamation. "Enough said. Next time you'll know better. I'm surprised that Sara didn't have the sense to explain these things to you, Mari. But James certainly should have known better." She turned her censorious gaze on him. Then with a final sniff, Martha grabbed her shopping cart and walked out the doors to the parking lot.

Mari looked at James and saw that he was pressing his lips tightly together to keep from laughing out loud. "Shh," she warned. Then she giggled. It really wasn't funny. Martha would tell everyone she knew, and probably people she didn't, that she had seen Mari and James having ice cream alone together. But seeing James laugh made it hard for Mari not to laugh.

Her groceries in one arm, he tugged on her coat sleeve and led her outside and around to where they'd left Jericho and the buggy parked.

"Stop laughing," she told him under his breath. "She'll tell Mattie, and then you'll be in trouble."

"I won't be in trouble." He took her hand to help her up into the buggy and leaned close to whisper in her ear. "But *you* certainly will be," he teased.

She sat down on the buggy seat, but he was still holding her hand. He leaned in so no one walking past them could overhear. "You're the one leading me astray, remember? First you sold me pork chops, unchaperoned, and now this."

Mari looked down at James and was so overwhelmed by the feel of his hand and his closeness that she suddenly felt dizzy. And happy. And guilty and scared and bold, all at the same time. "Get in the buggy," she whispered. "Before she comes back and insists on riding home with us."

He took one look at her and burst into laughter. She pushed him away playfully. "Get in the buggy."

He put her bag in the back and climbed up onto the seat beside her. As he picked up the reins, he leaned close to Mari and said, with a straight face, "Seven Poplars is *not* Hollywood."

And then they both burst out laughing.

"Seriously," James said as he guided his horse out onto the roadway. "Don't let her upset you. Like I told you before, it may not seem like it, but Martha means well. And until you've been properly chastised by Martha, you haven't really become part of the community."

Mari wiped away the tears of laughter from the corners of her eyes, liking the idea that he now considered her part of his community. "Are we really supposed to be chaperoned to ride to the grocery store?"

"Only in Martha's mind. Neither of us is sixteen. And you're not even Amish. Of course if we *were* courting—" he looked at her "—I suppose we'd have to follow at least some of the rules."

Mari suddenly felt self-conscious and pretended to be absorbed in rewrapping her wool scarf. She couldn't tell if James was being serious or not. And, worse, she didn't know which she preferred.

Chapter Nine

When Mari climbed out of the van Friday afternoon, she was so excited that she didn't mind splashing through the half thawed, half frozen muddy yard to reach Sara's back door. She removed her coat and boots, left them in the utility room and hurried to find her son.

Ellie and Sara were in the kitchen making supper, and she gave them a hearty greeting. "Good news on the school situation," Mari announced. "I can't believe it. Zachary's records finally arrived. The school called me at work. I can take him in Monday morning and enroll him."

"I know you're relieved." Ellie's enthusiasm was lackluster. "But I'll miss him, and I know his friends at our school will miss having him there." She went back to peeling potatoes.

Sara laid down her rolling pin, brushed flour off her apron and offered a polite smile. "Good news, indeed."

"Where is Zachary?" Mari glanced around. The sound of hammering came from the other end of the house, and she knew the answer. "I suppose he's trailing James around again?"

"Lots done today," Sara observed. "The plumber hooked up the water in the bathrooms, and James's crew is going to start on the drywall on Monday. It won't be long before they'll be moving on to a new job. I'll be glad to have it done, but I have to admit, I'll miss the crew."

"I think we all will," Ellie said, eyeing Mari, a certain sparkle in her eyes. "Some more than others."

Mari looked at Sara and then back at Ellie. "You mean me?"

Now Ellie was grinning. "Guess who stopped by during lunch today to drop off a donation of spiral notebooks and pencils?"

Mari shook her head, but she could feel her cheeks getting warm. She had a feeling she knew what Ellie was going to say.

"Martha Coblenz."

"That was nice of Martha to donate to the school," Mari said.

"Sure was." Ellie turned to her, a potato in one hand, a peeler in the other. "She told me a crazy story about running into a couple at Byler's store. A couple who she felt should have had a chaperone. She took me to task for not being there."

"Why would Martha—" Mari clasped her hands together. "I'm sorry, Ellie. I didn't mean to get you into trouble. James and I, we just…" She stopped and started again. She knew her entire face must be bright red. She really didn't feel as if she and James had done anything wrong. It wasn't as if they had been holding hands. Then she remembered him helping her into his buggy and holding her hand as he'd whispered to her and her face got warmer. "He gave me a ride home and his sister needed sugar and—"

Ellie laughed. "It's all right, Mari. I'm just teasing you. Actually, I'm pleased you and James caught Martha's attention. She brought me so many new pencils that every student in the school got two."

"Poor Martha," Sara sighed. "Now that Addy's happily married and out of the house, she's looking for people to fuss with."

Mari looked to Sara. "We didn't do anything wrong, did we?"

Sara shook her head. "You're not teenagers. So long as you behave yourselves and don't do anything couples have been known to do, there's nothing wrong with riding with James in his buggy or getting me half-and-half at Byler's." She took a sharp knife and began to cut the dough on the table into long strips. "We do like to keep an eye on young folks courting, just because... Well, as my grandmother used to say, little lambs will play. But both of you are nearly thirty. I think you know what's acceptable and what's not."

Mari lowered her voice, afraid James or one of the other men might hear her. "But we're not a couple."

"Of course you're not, dear." Sara didn't look up. "You should probably tell Zachary the good news and let him know it will soon be time to wash up for supper."

"Tell Zach we're having one of his favorites, chicken and slippery dumplings," Ellie called after her.

Mari found her son halfway up the staircase of the new addition, holding a can of nails for James. "Hi there," she said. She leaned down and kissed the crown of his head.

Zachary made a face, but his protest was only half-hearted. "Aw, Mom. Not in front of the guys."

James turned his face away, but she caught the hint of a mischievous smile. "You look as though you had a good day," he said. His words came out slightly garbled because he was holding several finishing nails between his lips. He set one in place and drove it home with several well-placed blows of his hammer. Above the step where he was working, unfinished planks had provided a way up and down for the workmen, but now that the addition was almost done, he was replacing them with furniture-grade oak.

"I did have a good day." Mari looked up at him. "The stair treads are beautiful. Almost too pretty to walk on."

"I was fortunate that Sara had some oak left over from her hospitality barn project. Wide boards. They're hard to find anymore because most of the old growth timber was cut years ago. But the grain on this is beautiful." He ran his fingertips lovingly across the surface of the stair tread he was nailing in place. Without being asked, Zachary held out three more nails. James nailed them in place, one after another. Then he stood and rubbed the small of his back. "We had a good day, too, didn't we, Zachary? After he got home from school, he did some sweeping for me and now we've got this staircase project."

"See what James is doing, Mom? He's sinking the nails, and he'll fill the holes with wooden pegs. And when you stain and varnish it, they'll show up in a different shade and look cool."

"I see," she said. "I'm sure they will. And I have something cool to share with you, too. Your school records have arrived, so Monday morning you start at the new elementary school."

Zachary frowned. "Mom, we need to talk." He looked down. "I've thought about it and…I don't want to go to that school."

"Zachary, we talked about this. You have to go to school. You're too young to join James's work crew."

He glanced at James. "Yeah, James and me, we talked about that. I understand I have to go to school. I just don't want to go to that English school. I like Ellie's school. I don't want to leave my friends."

"Zachary." She exhaled in exasperation. He was wearing a blue hand-sewn Amish shirt and suspenders, much like the clothing that James and the other men were wearing. First he'd starting wearing Amish pants because they had better pockets. Then James had bought him a pair of work boots, just for on the job. Now Mari couldn't remember the last time she saw him in one of his own sweatshirts. She wasn't even sure where he'd gotten the pale green long-sleeved shirt he was wearing today. Sara, maybe. "I don't know what to say."

James began to hammer another nail down.

Zachary dropped down a step. "Mom, please? I really like Ellie's school."

She leaned on the rail. Never in a hundred years had she been expecting *this* conversation. A week ago, he hadn't wanted to go with Ellie for the day. Now he was talking about attending full-time? "Honey, you can't really go there. It's just for Amish children. Parents pay for their children to attend."

"But Ellie's the best teacher I've ever had." Zachary looked up at her with hopeful eyes. "I really like it there.

Ellie explains stuff when I don't understand it. And the fourth grade is doing harder math than I was doing at my old school. It's fun. And I got a B on my test today."

"You took a test?"

Zachary nodded. "Yeah, and I got a B and I even helped Dora. She's in the fourth grade, but she's only doing third-grade multiplication. Ellie says it's okay if I help her with something if she needs it. Ellie says kids learn at different speeds."

"So you haven't just been helping Ellie?" she asked. "You're actually doing the lessons?"

"You're not mad, are you?" Zachary looked down at his dirty palms. "I didn't tell you because I thought you'd be mad. It's pretty neat, for school. At lunchtime we play games and do stuff together. And I get to carry in wood for the stove. They've got a woodstove right in the middle of the school. When you come in and your feet are cold, you prop them up on the railing and it's really toasty. And Ellie has cocoa on the stove. Anybody can have it. But only one cup a day because too much chocolate is bad for your teeth."

Mari sighed, glancing over her shoulder. "It sounds as if Ellie and I need to have a talk."

"Maybe you could ask her if I could stay?" Zachary begged. "It's so much fun there. The guys are neat, and nobody makes fun of anyone."

Mari pushed back a lock of hair that had fallen from her scarf. This was one of the hardest things about being a single parent—trying to do what was right with no one to talk to. She glanced up at James, who was now sitting on a step looking down at her. "What do *you* think?" she asked.

"It sounds to me as though you and Ellie do need

to talk," James said. "And she would need to discuss it with the school board, but…Zach does seem to be doing well."

"You don't think I should send him to the school in Dover?"

"I think you should follow your instincts," James said softly, holding her gaze.

For a moment, Mari felt as if it were just the two of them alone. Just her and James. They weren't touching; he was four steps above her. But she felt as though he were resting his hand on her shoulder.

"My instincts," she repeated softly.

Zachary looked at her, then at James and then at her again. "So, it's okay? I can stay at Ellie's school?" he asked.

"I'll think about it. Maybe…" She lowered her gaze to her son again. "Maybe it might be the best thing, letting you finish out the year with Ellie. And then we can talk about starting at the public school in the fall. Especially if you can keep up with the fourth-grade work and be able to go on to the fifth in September. What do you think, James?" She looked up at him again.

"I think it might be a good solution," he replied, gathering his hammer and the can of nails. "I guess I'd best be getting on home. Mattie will have supper started, and I've got the cow to milk before we eat."

"Can I go tell Ellie?" Zachary asked her. "Not that I can definitely go to her school, but that you're going to think about it? I know she'd be happy to talk to you."

Mari sighed and smiled. He looked so happy. "Go talk to her, but the three of us are going to sit down together and have a talk, too."

She and James watched Zachary bound down the stairs and out of the addition into the main house.

Mari turned back to James, who was still standing on the staircase above her. "Thank you, James."

"No need to thank me," he assured her, coming down the steps. "It's always good when people who care about each other can talk things out."

She headed down ahead of him.

"Are you going to the birthday supper for Hannah's mother-in-law tomorrow?" James asked.

"Sure am. Anna stopped by the butcher shop and invited us all to come. I don't think Sara can make it, but Zachary and I can walk."

"Thomas said he's taking Ellie. Mattie and I and the kids are going. We'd be glad to have you and Zachary ride with us."

"Are you certain we'll all fit in your buggy?"

He grinned. "The more the merrier. Besides, if you come along, I won't have to drive with one of the twins in my lap. You can hold him."

She laughed with him. "I'd be glad to come with you," she said. And then she just stood there for a moment looking at him. *He's the best friend I've ever had,* she thought. *Better than any man I've ever known. I trust him to do what he says he'll do. And he's been so good to Zachary.*

"Good," James said.

She started to turn away, then looked back at him. "Oh, I almost forgot. Guess who paid Ellie a visit today to tell her about her trip to Byler's Wednesday?"

"Martha." James chuckled. "I knew it."

"James, she thinks we're dating. One of us is going to have to say something to her."

He hung his hammer on his belt. "Why's that?"

"Because she's going to tell people we're…you know. Courting. And—"

"And we're not," he said softly. Then he met her gaze and held it.

It was a strange moment, standing there in the addition, alone, her looking at him, him looking at her. As if there was something else to be said, but she couldn't think what it could be.

"See you tomorrow, James," she finally said, making herself walk away.

"See you tomorrow, Mari."

Sara sat at the desk in her office off the living room going over the letter of a young woman from an Amish community in Wisconsin. Sara prided herself on making marriages in difficult cases, but this one in particular was going to be a challenge. The contact had come from the girl herself, which was unusual since she lived with her parents. Usually a close member of the family initiated the arrangements. In this case, there was a serious medical problem, one that might be inherited by future children.

The obvious solution would be to arrange a union with an older widower who already had children. But the writer stated plainly that she wanted to have a child and would only consider a husband who accepted the possibility of a child with health issues and was willing to leave the outcome to the Lord. Sara wasn't sure how she felt about that. Was the young woman being selfish and irresponsible? It was an issue Sara felt she needed to pray on and maybe seek the advice of Bishop Atlee or possibly their preacher, Caleb Wittner.

A hesitant knock sounded at the door. Sara folded the letter, put it back into the envelope and slid it into her desk drawer. *"Ya?"*

The door opened slowly, and Sara saw Zachary standing there. "Ready, are you?" she asked.

The evening before, he'd asked her for an appointment. "It's important," the boy had whispered. "Don't tell anybody. It's *confidential*."

"Well, come in," she said, her curiosity piqued. "And close the door behind you."

Zachary's features were set in a serious expression, and for a moment she wondered if he'd gotten into some mischief and was trying to fess up. But as his attire registered, Sara realized that it was something else. Zachary had slicked back his unruly hair and put on the Sunday go-to-meeting white shirt and black coat she'd dug up for him. He was still wearing jeans, but she remembered that Mari had thrown Zachary's good pants into the wash that morning on her way out the door to do her Saturday-morning shift. The boy was carrying a quart canning jar with what appeared to be dollar bills stuffed inside.

Sara sat up straight, swallowed her amusement at his attempt to appear manly and regarded him with as much dignity as she could muster. "This must be important," she said. "Would you like to sit down?"

Zachary glanced around uneasily, then nodded and slid onto a straight-backed chair directly across from her desk. His lips were pinched tightly together; his eyes fixed on her.

After a moment of silence, she said, "So you have something you want to talk to me about?"

He nodded.

She waited.

"I want to hire you to…make a match," he said, all in a rush.

"I see." She nodded gravely. "Don't you think you're a little young yet to be thinking about finding a wife?" She liked Zachary and she didn't want to hurt his feelings, but it was all she could do to hide her amusement.

He shook his head. "Not for me. For my mom." He held out the canning jar. Cobwebs clung to the outside, and Sara guessed that he'd just retrieved his stash from the barn loft or the recesses of the cellar. "I can pay your fee. I've got money." He pressed his lips together. "It's mine. What I earned working for James. I wanted to help pay for a car, but…" He straightened his thin shoulders. "I don't think we need a car. We get along just fine here without one."

"So you're here to discuss a business arrangement?"

"Yeah, I mean…*ya*." Zachary nodded again. "I'm not sure how this is supposed to work." He placed his money jar on the floor by his left shoe. "This Amish stuff is pretty new to me."

"Well, when talking with a client, I usually start by having some refreshments. Would you like hot chocolate?"

"What are you drinking?" He glanced at her mug.

"Coffee."

"Then I'll have coffee, if it's okay."

"If you like." She held out her cup. "There's a pot on the stove in the kitchen. Refill mine and pour one for yourself. Lots of milk."

In no time, Zachary was back with two cups of coffee on a little wooden tray they kept hanging on the wall in the kitchen for just that purpose. "I put lots of milk and sugar in mine," he explained as he set the tray down on her desk and picked up his mug.

She motioned for him to sit. "Tell me about this match you'd like me to arrange."

"Everybody says that you're the best, and…and you're the only matchmaker I know." Zachary glanced down at the jar. "I don't know how much it costs, but I've got twenty-one dollars and eleven cents. If it's more than that, I can pay some every week."

"Let's set the finances aside for a moment." She removed her glasses and used the corner of her apron to clean them, a ploy she often used to give herself a moment to think of what to say. "Who would you like me to find a match for?"

"My mom," he blurted. "So we can stay here."

"I see." Sara reached for her coffee mug. "Have you thought this over carefully? You haven't been here at Seven Poplars all that long. And you're really just getting settled in our school. Are you certain you can be happy here?"

"Yeah. I think so. I mean…" He frowned. "I like Ellie and the school, and the kids are cool. Especially Jonah and 'Kota and J.J."

"You told your mother that you wanted to go back to Wisconsin. Have you changed your mind about that?"

"Yeah." He hesitated. "I like the stuff we do here. Working. And the horses. And we all play games at recess. Nobody pushes you around."

"Did people push you around at your old school?"

Zachary grimaced. "I'm not as big as some kids my age. At our old school, some guys thought they were all that. They took my coat, the one I told Mom disappeared. One of the older kids ran away with it."

"But you didn't tell a teacher?"

He shook his head. "Being a squealer could get you hurt. Everybody would gang up on you on the playground. I was scared of getting beat up."

"I'm sorry to hear that," Sara said. "But you should have told your mother."

"I guess."

"Does this happen at Ellie's school?"

He shook his head again. "No way. The bigger guys help you out. Peter showed me how to hold a baseball bat, and I got a hit. We were all playing ball after school yesterday." He wrinkled his nose. "It was a little slushy, but we didn't care."

She smiled. "I'm glad that this school is working out for you, Zachary. Amish don't believe in fighting. We don't believe in violence at all."

"That's what Mom said. She says Amish people are…gentle. It's why I want you to get a husband for her. So we can stay here."

Sara pursed her lips. She'd not expected this. But Zachary seemed serious, and she didn't want to hurt his feelings. "You understand that the matches I make are all for Old Order Amish couples," she said carefully. "Do you think your mother would want to marry an Amish man?"

"Maybe she would. I *think* she would. If we found her a good one. She likes it here."

Sara nodded thoughtfully. "And if I find her an Amish husband, she'd have to join the church herself. She'd be Amish. And so would you. How would you feel about that?"

"Me, too?"

Sara nodded again. "You wouldn't be expected to

join the church now. That's for adults. But you would have to go to church regularly. Can you do that?"

Zachary slid forward on his chair and balanced his mug on one knee. "It was okay. I think I could." He took a sip of the coffee and puckered his mouth.

"Maybe a little more milk," Sara suggested, pointing to a small pitcher on the corner of her desk. "And another sugar lump. It's a big cup."

"Thanks." Zachary carried his cup to the table and helped himself to both. He used the spoon to stir it and tasted the coffee.

"Better?" Sara asked. She'd never seen Zachary drink coffee before.

Zachary dropped in another cube of sugar. "This is good," he said. And then he added more milk.

"So you're okay with having an Amish father?" she asked.

"Yeah." He grimaced. "I hate moving to new schools. In second grade we moved twice. It's weird, you know. You don't know anybody. If Mom gets married to an Amish man, I can just stay at Ellie's school."

"I imagine moving has been hard on you."

He nodded. "Sometimes. But it's tough for my mom, too. Getting up the rent and money for electric." He offered a little smile. "No electricity bill if you're Amish."

Sara toyed with her glasses, rubbing a finger along the rim. "And how does your mom like the idea of an Amish husband? Do you think she'd agree if I found her a good match?"

"Oh, I've already picked out the guy for her. I just need you to convince her to marry him."

Sara raised her eyebrows. She had liked Zachary the night he'd arrived, cranky and tired, but with every passing day, she liked him more. It was almost as if he was becoming the grandson she didn't have. "So this is all your idea?"

He nodded.

"And you haven't talked with your mother about a husband?"

He shook his head.

"I see." She didn't see at all. Lilly's cousin's mother had made an inquiry about Mari on behalf of her son Calvin, but the woman had quickly cooled when Sara had explained that Mari hadn't been baptized yet. She'd mentioned it to Mari, who'd chuckled and said that it was just as well because she wasn't certain she knew how to cook duck. It had seemed an odd reply, but Mari and Ellie had both laughed until tears rolled down their cheeks. So Mari definitely wasn't interested in the duck farmer. Who, then, did Zachary have in mind?

"You can't guess who I mean?" Zachary set his cup of coffee, barely touched, on a table beside his chair. "James, of course. He likes her. I know he does."

Sara lifted her brows, pleasantly surprised, not so much by the statement but by the boy's keen observation. *Out of the mouths of babes*... "James likes your mother?"

"Yeah." Zachary eyed an oatmeal cookie on a plate on her desk. "I just don't know if *she* knows. He looks at her all the time when she's not looking at him. And he smiles a lot when she's around."

"And you think they'd be a good match? Your mother and James?" She handed him the cookie, left over from her midmorning snack.

Zachary took a big bite. "They like to be together,

and she always asks him about stuff. James doesn't have a wife. And he needs one."

"He does?" Sara asked. "And why is that?"

"Because Mattie is moving into her own house and James will be all alone. He might be scared there by himself." He stuffed the rest of the cookie into his mouth. "And he wouldn't have anybody to eat with him and stuff." Zachary folded his arms over his chest. "I could help him, too. With his carpentry stuff and taking care of Jericho. James is teaching me how to drive. And if I was his son, he wouldn't have to pay me, and he'd have more money. So it would be better for both him and Mom." He looked down at the floor and slid one foot back and forth. "So what do you think? Will you do it?"

Sara smiled. "I think something can be arranged."

Chapter Ten

James came for Mari and Zachary on Saturday as he'd promised, and Mari felt a warm glow of excitement as his buggy stopped near Sara's back door. She and Zachary donned their coats and hurried out to discover that James was alone. "Your sister didn't come with you?"

"Emanuel and Roman both have upset stomachs," James explained as he came around the back to help Mari into the buggy. "Zach, you scoot up on the bench and sit between us," he said. "I promised to teach you the basics of driving, and this is as good a time as any to start."

"Yes!" Zachary fist-pumped.

"I'm sorry the kids are sick." Mari took James's warm hand and stepped up easily, settling herself on the cushioned seat. Amish buggies were all supposed to be alike, but they rarely were. Some, like their owners, were sparse, dusty and needed sprucing up, while others boasted black leather seats, an oiled dashboard and a spotless interior. There were no fancy red, white and blue blinking lights or extras visible inside James's vehicle, but the buggy had obviously been cleaned and recently painted inside.

"Mattie was disappointed to miss Lovina's birthday party," he said, "but Roman and Emanuel spent the afternoon sick to their stomachs. She could hardly inflict that on Anna and her guests."

"I hope the babies don't get sick, too."

"I doubt it's a virus," James confided. "I think the problem might be related to a jar of oatmeal cookies they got into while their mother was changing diapers."

Mari couldn't help laughing. "Those boys are a handful."

"That they are. The twins will have a high bar to get over if they want to match them for mischief. But Mattie has gone to so much trouble getting Roman and Emanuel to this age that I suppose she'll have to keep them."

Zachary, now sitting between them, glanced up at James, a worried look on his face.

"He's teasing," Mari assured her son. "Mattie loves all her children."

"She does," James agreed with a grin. "I think she even loves me, and when I was Roman's age, I was worse than he is, if you can believe what Mattie says. She was a good big sister, and she's a wonderful mother. She's smart and she's kindhearted. Women like that aren't easy to find."

"My mom's smart," Zach piped up, looking at James. "You could marry her, and then I could drive Jericho all the time."

Mari could feel the heat rising from her neck upward. Mortified, she didn't know what to say. As she opened her mouth to force something out, James laughed and tousled Zach's hair. "Now, that's an idea," he said, grinning as he pressed the reins into her son's hands. "This is how you hold the leathers. You have to be gentle but firm."

Mari looked away, touching her hand to her cheek. She had to be bright red with embarrassment. "So Lovina lives with Anna and her husband, doesn't she?" she asked. She knew very well that Lovina did, but she felt desperate to move the conversation to safer ground.

"She's been living with them for a while." James gently adjusted the reins in Zach's hands again. "That's right. Like that."

Mari had learned from Sara that Lovina Yoder, Hannah's first mother-in-law, had moved in with Hannah when she gave up her home in Ohio and moved to Seven Poplars. But the two never got on well. Anna was Lovina's favorite granddaughter and the only one with whom she never found fault. Apparently, Lovina was happier in Anna's home, and Anna and Samuel insisted that they loved having her with them.

"Lovina's strong-willed, as is Anna, so they're well suited to each other," James went on. "Everyone thinks it's a good solution." And then to Zachary, he said, "We call the reins *leathers*. You hold them firmly, but you don't jerk them or you'll hurt the horse's mouth. Jericho has a tender mouth, but he's a smart horse and eager to please. Not all animals are so easy to drive, but you need to treat them all with respect, even the difficult ones."

"James, you don't have to do this today," Mari said. "You could teach him another day, just around the farm." They'd be traveling on the paved road with motor traffic once they reached the end of the drive, and Zachary knew nothing of horses.

"Mom," her son protested. "I can do it. Peter and Rudy both drive on the road."

"Samuel's sons are older than you are," she answered. "I'm sure they weren't taking their parents' buggy on the road at age nine."

"This will be a short lesson today. Just until we get to the end of the lane." James nodded his approval. "That's it. Good grip. Now give him the order to 'walk on.'"

"Walk on," Zachary said, and he gave an excited sigh of delight when the horse obeyed.

Mari watched the serious way Zachary held the reins and felt a distinctly un-Amish pride in his first attempt at driving.

"That's right," James encouraged. He didn't touch the reins himself, but Mari saw that he was watching Zachary closely. "Good," James said. "You have a steady hand. Never let a horse know when you're frightened or unsure of yourself because they'll pick up on it and act accordingly."

"Addy said that Lovina is her grandmother, as well?" Mari asked, starting to relax. James didn't seem to be the least upset by Zach's remark.

"Yes, Lovina is Martha's mother. All right, Zach. I'll take over now." James took the reins, and Zachary dropped his hands into his lap.

"When can I drive again?" her son asked eagerly.

"Soon, I promise." James waited until a car passed and then eased the horse and buggy onto the blacktop.

With James driving, Mari felt herself relax. "Anna lives near the school, doesn't she?"

"Yeah, Mom," Zachary answered. "Right next door, just through the woods. Peter and Rudy just walk over.

Most of the kids walk, and if I didn't ride with Ellie, I could walk, too."

Mari was still weighing the pros and cons of Zachary attending the Amish school, at least long-term as he was pushing for. She'd discussed it with Ellie at length and mulled it all over in her mind. But considering that Zachary wanted to go and was applying himself, she couldn't think of a good reason to forbid it.

Since the Mast home was near Sara's, less than two miles away, it didn't take long to reach it. Mari could smell food as she climbed down from the buggy. "You go on in," James told her. "Zachary and I will tie up Jericho."

Rebecca saw her as she walked toward the house, waved and hurried to welcome her. "I'm so glad you could come." Rebecca gave Mari a hug. "We're going to eat soon. Anna baked a huge pineapple cake, and *Grossmama* can't stop talking about it. She loves cake."

The warmth of the big farmhouse, even larger and finer than Hannah's, overflowing with relatives, friends and neighbors, enveloped Mari as Rebecca led her inside. Guests nodded, smiled and called out greetings to Mari and others who filed in behind her. The elderly Lovina was holding court in a high-backed, old-fashioned, cushioned chair near the woodstove that stood in one corner of the combination kitchen and dining room. Mari could see that the aging matron had once been tall and slim. Now she was rail-thin, her nose a sharp beak and her back bent, but her eyes as fierce as any hawk's.

When Mari went to say hello, Lovina peered at her through her wire-rim glasses. "You have the look of your *grossmama*," she pronounced in a raspy voice when Mari greeted her.

Sara had warned Mari that Lovina's memory often failed her and that she suffered from early-stage dementia, but this white-*kapped* woman with the iron-gray hair who was sizing her up seemed alert and shrewd.

"*Grossmama*, this is Mari Troyer, Sara's friend," Rebecca introduced. "She's from Wisconsin."

"I know who she is." Lovina spoke in *Deitsch*. She stared hard at Mari. "You're Maryann Troyer's granddaughter."

Mari's mouth gaped in surprise. "You knew my grandmother Maryann?"

"Pfff, and why wouldn't I know her? We were second cousins. Grew up next door to each other. I've known Maryann since we were both in leading strings. She was Maryann Stutz then. She married some boy from Wisconsin and went off to live with his family."

Rebecca took a step closer. Someone passed her a plate of food. She placed it on the small table beside Lovina's chair and arranged a knife, fork and spoon where the elderly woman could reach it. "You and Mari's grandmother are cousins?"

Lovina scowled at her. "Didn't I just say we were? Second cousins, if you want to slice the ham close to the bone, but blood kin, all the same. So this skinny little thing from Wisconsin is family. Not only on my side, but on the Yoder side, as well. Double kin to you and your sisters. Maryann's people settled in the valley two hundred years ago." The beady eyes turned on Mari. "Glad you've had the sense to finally come to Delaware. Did you bring your grandmother?"

Mari shook her head. "She passed on."

"I'm sorry to hear it, even if she has gone on to her reward. You have the look of Maryann, child. Welcome to my home." Lovina turned abruptly to inspect her plate of food. "Stingy with the gravy, weren't you, Rebecca?"

Mari could see the corners of Rebecca's mouth twitching with amusement. "Anna made your plate, *Grossmama*. Just the way you like it. And you said not to give you too much gravy because you needed to leave room for cake."

With the older folks' and the children's plates made, everyone else got into line to help themselves at the buffet table. "Was my grandmother really a cousin to Lovina?" Mari whispered in Rebecca's ear when they were far enough away that there was no chance of Lovina overhearing.

Rebecca shrugged. "She must have been. *Grossmama* gets confused about a lot of things, but never about family ties. Wait until our *mam* and Sara hear. They'll be delighted." Rebecca hugged her again. "And that makes us cousins, too. Welcome to the family."

"Thank you," Mari managed. She was almost too astonished to speak. *Family.* She had *family* here in Seven Poplars. It didn't matter that the connections were old ones. Among the Amish any relative was important. If Lovina was right, she was a cousin to Hannah's daughters and to Sara, as well. It didn't seem possible. She'd thought that she and Zachary were alone in the world, but here were more relatives than she could count.

"I think *Grossmama* likes you," Rebecca said as they joined the food line.

"You think so?" Mari asked. "How can you tell?"

Rebecca laughed. "Oh, if she didn't, she'd have let you know. She and Aunt Martha both have a way of laying all their wash on the table." She shook her head. "The good thing about being related to *Grossmama* is that Addy's your cousin." She rolled her eyes. "And the bad thing is that Aunt Martha is bound to try and find fault with you."

"Oh, she's already done that." Mari hesitated, not sure if she should tell Rebecca about her and James at Byler's, but she had a feeling that even if Martha hadn't shared with everyone in Seven Poplars yet, it was only a matter of time before the word spread. She kept her voice low. "James gave me a ride home from work the other day and we stopped at Byler's for a few things."

Rebecca grabbed Mari's forearm, amusement on her face. "And she caught you two alone together?"

"Eating ice cream," Mari confessed.

Rebecca giggled.

"But we were just sitting at the picnic tables. We weren't doing anything wrong."

Rebecca gave a wave of dismissal. "Pay her no mind. She has this idea that she needs to monitor all the couples in the county. Some of the young folks are calling her 'the courting police.'"

The line had moved forward, and it was almost their turn to fill their plates. "James and I aren't a couple," she whispered. "I don't understand why everyone keeps saying that. I'm not even Amish."

Rebecca waggled her finger. "According to Lovina, you are."

Mari sighed. "You know what I mean. I haven't lived this life in a very long time. I haven't been baptized."

Rebecca took Mari's hand and looked into her eyes. "Do you want to be baptized?" she asked softly.

"I don't know," Mari whispered. "I think maybe yes, but…" She closed her eyes for a moment. "Rebecca, I'm so confused. If I'm honest with myself, I think James and I—" She exhaled. *James and I what?* "I don't want to take this step for the wrong reasons. I need someone to tell me what to do."

Rebecca squeezed her hand and let it go. "No one can tell you what's right for you. You need to pray about it. And you need to talk to the bishop. Maybe he can help you figure out where God is leading you."

"You think so?" Mari asked, wanting desperately to believe her. "He'd be willing to talk to me?"

"Absolutely. Now turn around—" she pointed over Mari's shoulder "—and grab a piece of fried chicken for me before it's all gone."

The thought that the Yoders were family warmed Mari throughout the evening, and she was still smiling when James brought the buggy to Anna's back door. "We don't need to wait for Zach. He's spending the night here with Johanna's boys." She made a face. "*Ach*, I hadn't thought this through. I hope this won't cause talk, you taking me home."

"No worry," he said, walking around to adjust a buckle on Jericho's harness. "Everyone in Seven Poplars has already heard we've been to Byler's for ice cream alone. Martha told Anna Yoder that we were secretly walking out together." He winked at her. "We'll be doing Martha a service, giving her something else to talk about."

She smiled hesitantly back at him, trying to read his face. She knew, of course, that he was joking, but was there something more in his voice? Did he wish it were true? Or was that just her own wishful thinking?

Mari made no move to climb into the buggy; instead, she watched by the light of the gas lamppost as James unbuckled Jericho's harness to make an adjustment. She hadn't been kidding when she'd told Rebecca that she was confused. She was *so* confused. About everything. About how she felt about God and the church she'd grown up in. About how she felt about James. About her whole life and where she wanted to go from here. She'd come to Seven Poplars thinking she'd stay a few months, then get a nice trailer for Zachary and her. But now she didn't want that. She wanted more. She wanted to belong to a community. She even thought that she wanted a family of her own: a husband, more children.

"Did you have a good time this evening?" James asked, still working on the harness. "I didn't get a chance to talk to you."

"I did." She tightened the wool scarf she wore around her neck. "Lovina says that she and my grandmother were second cousins. I never knew that much about my mother's family because I was young when she died. But I do remember my grandmother Maryann telling me that she grew up on a farm in central Pennsylvania and that they'd been very poor."

"And how do you feel about that?" he asked. "Being related to the Yoders?"

"I think it's great. Wonderful. You probably don't realize what it's like because you have family all around you, but I really like the idea of belonging somewhere. Belonging *to* someone."

"I know exactly what you're saying. I was away for a long time, and there's nothing like that feeling of coming home…of being among your own."

"You do understand," she said. She was so excited that she was at a loss for words. "I've always thought that Zachary and I were all alone in the world, and now… It's a good feeling."

He nodded.

She hesitated and then went on, "I talked a little bit with Rebecca tonight about church and…she suggested I talk with Bishop Atlee. And I was wondering…" She gazed out into the snowy barnyard. "I was wondering if you thought that would be a good idea."

He turned around to face her. "Can I ask why you'd like to talk to him?"

She clasped her hands, looking into his dark eyes. "I…I feel like God is calling me back, but I… I don't know, James." She suddenly felt herself tearing up. "But I want to be sure I'm truly being called. I don't want to become a part of the church just so I can be a part of all this." She waved in the direction of the Mast house, where light danced from the windows and the sound of laughter drifted through an open door.

They were both quiet for a second. She couldn't read his face.

Finally James spoke. "I think that talking to Bishop Atlee might be a very good idea. He can help you work your way through things. Pray with you. When I first came back, he was a lot of help. He has a good perspective. We did a lot of praying together."

Mari felt as though she couldn't breathe. She and James weren't touching, but the way he was looking at her made her feel as if he had wrapped his arms around her. His name rested on her lips, but she didn't say it.

"We should go," he said.

She nodded, turning to face the buggy, her emotions all a jumble. The decision had been made. She was going to talk to the bishop. But the decision to do it felt good. It felt right.

"I'd be happy to make the arrangements with the bishop for you," James offered. "He could come to Sara's, and you could talk in private in her office."

Mari reached up to grab the handhold on the buggy to step up, and he surprised her by coming up behind her, putting his hands around her waist and lifting her up. As she dropped onto her seat, her hand caught his. It was completely by accident, but then he squeezed it before letting go.

The intimacy of the gesture made her light-headed. She found herself surprised again by her own reaction. It had been a long time since she'd felt this way when a man touched her, almost too long to remember.

Flustered, she sat there in the moonlight, looking down at his kind, gentle face.

At that moment she felt as if he was going to say something, but then he turned and walked around the buggy to get in on his side.

It was still very cold as Jericho trotted down the driveway, but Mari didn't feel the chill because the memory of James's touch warmed her and filled her with a bubbly happiness.

Chapter Eleven

"Mari, could you give me a hand?" Sara asked. They had finished the last of the supper dishes and Ellie and Zachary were bent over a math problem at the kitchen table. "I want to take these extra jars of pickled green tomatoes down to the cellar and bring up applesauce and green beans for tomorrow."

"Sure. I'd be glad to help." Mari hung the dish towel over the handle of the woodstove and went to the counter to pick up a box of canned goods. "I know you didn't can tomatoes yesterday."

Sara shook her head. "No. Gideon brought them by. Careful with the steps. They're steep." She opened the door that led down to the cellar from the utility area off the kitchen.

The cellar was cool and dry with rows of metal shelving along two walls. Canned vegetables and fruits were neatly arranged in allotted sections, and there were wooden bins for potatoes, sweet potatoes, cabbages and turnips. "You could feed an army with all this food," Mari remarked.

"I hope not an army. But I could host more than a

few community doings." When they placed the jars in
their proper places and found the green beans and applesauce for the next day, Sara motioned to the long
table in the center of the room. Benches ran on either
side. "I was looking for an opportunity to talk with you
alone," she explained. "I could ask you to my office,
but that might have Ellie or Zachary wondering what
business we're up to."

Curious, Mari took a seat.

Sara patted her hand reassuringly. "What I wanted
to discuss with you isn't a complaint, so don't look so
worried. It's an opportunity. But I'd like to ask something personal of you first."

Mari looked at her expectantly. "Of course." She
smiled. "We're family, remember?"

Sara smiled back. "Your meetings with the bishop?
Have they gone well?"

Mari folded her hands and placed them on the table.
She was so glad that Rebecca had suggested she talk to
Bishop Atlee and that James had been willing to make
the arrangements for her. She didn't know if she would
have been brave enough to do it on her own. As promised, Bishop Atlee had been wonderful at helping her
work through not only her past feelings about church
but her expectations for the future. She met Sara's gaze
across the table. "They've gone very well."

"I suspected so. You've seemed so happy lately."
Sara's dark eyes caught the light from the overhead
fixture and shone with compassion. "I don't mean to
pry. But whether or not you decide to return to the faith
has great bearing on the proposition I have to present
to you."

Mari stared at Sara across the table. "I don't understand."

"Someone, I'm not at liberty to say who, has come to me to request that I arrange a match for you with a man here in Seven Poplars."

"A match for me?" She knew her eyes must have grown as wide as saucers. "With an Amish man?"

"Of course. It's the only sort of marriage proposals I arrange."

"But…how could you… How could I…" She let out a breath that she hadn't realized she'd been holding. "I'm not Amish."

"Exactly. As I said, my proposal is contingent on your deciding to attend classes with the bishop with the intention of baptism into the Amish faith." Sara placed both elbows on the table and linked the fingers of both hands. "If you haven't considered returning to the church, then what I'm proposing is impossible. And my intention isn't to influence you. Marriage shouldn't be a reason for accepting our faith. It must be a call from God, and it must be deep and sincere."

A shiver went through Mari, and she wrapped her arms around herself. "I can't tell you if I'm going to join the church because I don't know what I'm going to do."

"But you have considered it?"

"Yes." She nodded. "Yes, of course, I've thought of it. I've thought of it almost every day of my life since I left my uncle's home. More so since I've become a part of this community. But I'm not sure. I could never… would never ask for baptism under false pretenses. If I do become Amish again, it will be with all my heart. It won't be to get a husband."

"Good." Sara smiled, and her shoulders relaxed their stiffness. "That's what I wanted to hear you say."

Mari narrowed her gaze. "Who came to you about finding me a husband?"

"As I said, I can't tell you that."

Mari thought for a second, fighting a sense of panic. Her heart was pounding in her chest. She couldn't imagine who would think she needed an Amish husband. "Who does this secret someone think I should marry?"

"Why, James, of course."

"James wants to marry me?" she asked when she recovered her power of speech. "*He's* the one who proposed this match?"

"That's not what I said. The person who came to me feels that the two of you would make a good couple, that you would be right for each other and would make each other happy." Sara's gaze sharpened. "Am I not wrong in thinking that you aren't opposed to such a union?"

First Mari was dizzy, and then she felt slightly nauseated. What a ridiculous thing for her to say. Now she'd embarrassed herself in front of Sara. Of course James hadn't come asking for her hand in marriage. "James doesn't think of me that way," Mari managed. "He...he considers me a friend." She dared a peek at Sara's face. "James doesn't know about this, does he?"

"I haven't approached James. That's not the way it works. I always go to the woman first. But I wouldn't have come to you at all if I didn't think this was a possibility." Sara's tone grew tender. "Remember, dear, I've been doing this a long time."

"But marriage with James?" Mari felt dizzy with the thought of it. "I...I don't know what to say. We're friends, yes, but I..." She stared at the tabletop, her eyes wide. "I never thought that it was more than that with him."

"That's for James to say. Many a solid marriage has started with friendship. And respect. You do respect him, don't you?"

Mari lifted her gaze to meet Sara's. "Immensely. He's a wonderful person. He'd make a wonderful stepfather to Zachary, but…" She shook her head. "This is too much to take in. I haven't known him that long. And I don't know if I can…if I will join the church. It's a decision that doesn't affect just me—it's my son's life, too. It's such a big step, to leave the world and become Amish."

"Not so great a gap to bridge if it's God's plan for you. Ours isn't a life of sacrifice, so much as one of joy. I believe you can find happiness in the church…in our community. And I think it would give Zachary the sense of belonging that he's lacked."

Mari's thoughts were flying in a hundred directions at once. Marriage to James. It seemed too good to be true. This wasn't a decision that could be rushed. She'd learned that with Zachary's father. "I can't agree to marry a man so quickly…not even a man like James."

"Are you refusing to consider the match?" Sara asked, seemingly choosing her words precisely.

Mari shook her head. "I'm saying that I need more time." She hesitated. "How does this work? If I *was* interested, does that mean I'm committing to marry him?"

"Not at all. If you are open to a match with the designated person, then I go to him. If both agree, then you start walking out together. Just as you would if a matchmaker weren't involved. Neither of you would make any commitment until you were certain."

Suddenly, Mari's life seemed full of possibilities. But could she trust her feelings? "How...how much time is to be allotted for this courtship?"

"There's no time limit. I had one couple that took two years to decide."

"And did they marry?" Mari asked.

"No, they decided against it. Each later married other people, and both the man and woman are content." She smiled. "I made the new matches. I doubted that the first would work out from the beginning, but the girl's parents insisted that he was the one. Time and common sense proved them wrong. And we were all happy with the outcome. Marriage is a sacred bond. You must be sure."

"It's why I want to wait." Mari rose slowly, barely aware of the words she was speaking. Someone actually thought she and James would be well suited to marry. She couldn't help but be thrilled by the idea. Even if it wasn't possible, it did her heart good to know that she hadn't imagined how well she and James got along. "To have time to know my own mind."

"Then that's what I'll tell the person who approached me about matching you and James. We'll table this whole thing at the moment."

"And you won't say anything to James?" Mari asked.

"Of course not." Sara smiled. "But you will consider the offer, won't you?"

"I will," Mari promised.

Mari stepped off the blacktop into the grass as a pickup truck whooshed past. The driver honked the horn, but it didn't faze her. She was in too good a mood to let anyone annoy her. In her denim coat and wool scarf, she was warm, and after the week of working at the butcher shop, walking to and from Bishop Atlee's house was a pleasant change of pace. It felt good to be outside in the brisk air, getting exercise and having some time alone to think.

She'd had a good afternoon with Bishop Atlee. His gentle wisdom and absolute faith in the goodness and mercy of God did much to ease her mind. Every Saturday afternoon and Tuesday night, he'd reserved an hour for her, and with each visit, she'd become more certain that this might be the right path for her and Zachary.

Mari's church attendance and visits with the bishop gave her an inner calm and a joy in everyday life that she hadn't had in a long time. It should have been enough for anyone, but strangely it wasn't. Because while every aspect of Mari's life seemed to be falling into place, there was one piece of the puzzle she just couldn't figure out. And that was James. Sara had been true to her word and not mentioned the proposal again, but that didn't mean Mari didn't think about it. She knew she had done the right thing in telling Sara she wasn't ready to think about marriage, to anyone, but a part of her wished she was. A part of her wanted to marry James and have his babies.

Wanting James as a husband went against years of conviction that she didn't need a man. She had Zachary, and she was able to work and provide for herself and her son. She'd given her heart to Zachary's father, and he had broken it. The pain had been devastating. Why would she want to risk everything again? She'd had her chance and failed miserably because she'd been a terrible judge of character. Ivan had been weak. He'd thought more of himself than the child they'd brought into the world. Ivan had been unwilling to make the sacrifices necessary to make a marriage that would protect and nurture Zachary.

It was a good argument against mooning over James like some love-struck teenager, but it fell flat. James was a strong and good man. He'd proved his worth many times over. And she loved him. She was *in love* with him.

But what if James didn't feel the same way about her?

Mari sighed and loosened her scarf. She was spending too much time dwelling on James. She had other things to think about, like where she and Zachary were going to live. Even if she did join the church, she couldn't board permanently with Sara, could she?

She wanted to remain within walking distance of her friends and her newfound family and the bishop's house. If she officially began lessons with him to prepare to be baptized, they would run a full year before she could be considered for church membership. And it had to be a place that was affordable on her salary. Apparently, someone in the next church district over had an empty *dawdi* house on their property they might be willing to rent. It wouldn't be too long a walk, but—

Her thoughts strayed to James again. In her mind's eye, she pictured his sweet smile and heard the sound of his voice when he laughed or said her name. When she closed her eyes, she could almost smell the scents of fresh-cut lumber and oiled leather that lingered in the air around him. She could see the way his lean hands looked when he clasped Jericho's reins or held a hammer.

Unconsciously, Mari picked up her pace. Sara's addition was done, and James's crew had started to work on a new job. But James still made a practice of stopping by sometimes to have coffee with Sara and the family before work or coming by to finish up a few odds and ends at Sara's. The previous Saturday, after her meeting at Bishop Atlee's, she'd seen James's buggy in Sara's yard, and she couldn't help hoping he might have come again today.

As much as she loved being with Zachary and with Sara and Ellie, Mari always had things she wanted to tell James. She'd share her experiences at the butcher shop with him, and he would tell her community news or funny things that had occurred with his nephews. It was James she could talk to about how to deal with a difficult customer, and it was James who gave her good advice on dealing with Zachary when he got into mischief.

She turned into the driveway and walked a little faster. James wouldn't be there, she knew he wouldn't, but she couldn't help hoping—

"Mari!"

She gave a small gasp of delight as she heard James's voice as she came into full view of the house. "James!" she called back, spotting him on the porch.

He walked toward her.

"I was hoping you'd be here," she called.

"You're later today than last week." He stopped and smiled at her as she approached. "How did it go?"

"Hey, Mom!"

Mari glanced toward the barn and saw Zachary. He and J.J. were standing in the open door of the hayloft.

Zachary waved. "I'm showing J.J. the new kittens. Lois said I could. She's in the house." He pointed. "Sara said Lois could keep an eye on me and J.J. while she was gone. She said I didn't have to go with her."

Lois was a new girl staying with Sara now; Mari liked her very much and trusted her completely. Mari waved to J.J. Then she said to both boys, "Just don't frighten the mama cat or she'll move them again."

"We won't!" Zachary shouted.

Mari met James's amused gaze. "See, I'm trying," she said quietly so the boys didn't hear her. "I didn't warn him to be careful even though I wanted to. I just keep seeing him tumbling out of the loft and me rushing him to the emergency room."

James chuckled. "Didn't you ever play in a hayloft when you were a kid?"

"I did," she admitted. "It was a favorite spot for me and my girl cousins to play house."

"And you never fell out of the loft window?"

She shook her head. "No, I didn't, but it's different when it's my child. And boys do fall, and sometimes they get hurt."

His eyes filled with understanding. "They do, but it's part of growing up. You can't protect him from everything. You have to learn to trust Zach's judgment. He's got a pretty good head on his shoulders."

"I know he does," she agreed. She headed for the porch. "You have time to sit a minute, or are you on your way out?"

James settled onto the porch swing as she took the rocker across from him. "I always have time for you."

Chapter Twelve

Mari stood at the kitchen window, her coffee mug in her hand. Hiram had already gone to hitch the buggy to go to church services at Roman and Fanny Byler's, and she was just waiting for Sara and Ellie. Zachary had spent the night at Johanna and Roland's and would meet her at church.

Mari watched as a bit of straw blew across the yard. The last of the snow had melted and the first green shoots of spring were popping up everywhere. The day before she'd spotted crocuses at the mailbox. She thought about how cold it had been when she'd left Wisconsin; it had felt as though she would never see the sun again. But here it was, with the first warm rays of the coming spring.

Her life seemed to be transforming with the weather. A short time ago she'd been in Wisconsin with no job, no home and no real hope. Then she'd come to Seven Poplars and everything had changed. Sara and the whole community had made her and Zachary feel so welcome. Her job was great, and Zachary had settled in at the lit-tle Amish school, doing better than he'd ever done in a public school. And now she was taking classes with the bishop and making plans to join the church.

She was happier than she had ever dreamed she could be. And yet there was still something missing. In the past week Mari had twice almost spoken to Sara about the courtship with James proposed by the mysterious benefactor. Now that she had decided to join the church, it only made sense to let Sara try to make the match.

But there was a part of Mari that still held back. She had no doubts about her feelings for James. She knew she loved him; with each passing day that became more evident. And even though they were both content to call each other "friend," she knew that he had feelings for her, as well. But what if it was all her imagination? What if Sara went to him and proposed the courtship and he said no?

The truth was, she was madly in love with James.

Which made her question her decision to join the church. What if somehow, subconsciously, she was thinking she felt God's love, when it was James's love she sought?

From somewhere in the house, Ellie's and Sara's voices drifted down. Mari was dressed for church in a beautiful blue dress Sara had made for her in the Amish style. She wasn't wearing a prayer *kapp* yet, but Sara had made her a scarf in matching blue fabric. With dark stockings and black leather shoes and her hair up under the scarf, no Englisher would have known she wasn't Amish.

Suddenly she felt overwhelmed. What if she was just playing dress-up? What if God wasn't really calling her? What if she was going to church and meeting with the bishop just because of James? What if she was wrong about her newfound faith?

Footsteps sounded in the living room: Sara's followed by Ellie's.

"Ready," Sara called.

When Sara walked into the kitchen, Mari backed up to the sink. Suddenly she didn't fell so well.

"We should go. Hiram's waiting," Sara said as she crossed the kitchen.

"Oh, good." Ellie tied on her black bonnet over her prayer *kapp* as she hurried behind Sara. "He's already loaded the vegetable soup and brownies. The soup will go well on a chilly spring day like this." She caught Mari's eye and halted. "Are you feeling all right?"

Mari pressed her hand to her forehead. "Actually... I don't think I am."

"Oh, dear." Sara sighed, throwing her black cloak over her shoulders. "That's the downside to working in a store. So many people. So many germs."

Ellie frowned, looking at Mari. "Do you think you have a fever? You look flushed."

"I..." Mari lowered her hand. "I don't think so, but I think I better stay home. Just in case," she added, feeling a little guilty. While she did feel light-headed and flushed, she knew it wasn't from a bug she'd caught at the store. "Will you just bring Zachary home with you this afternoon?"

Sara stood in the doorway, watching her closely. "Of course. But one of us can stay here with you, if you like."

"Oh no. I'll be fine." She waved them off. "I wouldn't want you to miss service on my account. Go, and tell everyone I said hello."

Sara met Mari's gaze and Mari had to fight the urge to squirm. She really didn't feel as if she could go to church this morning. Her thoughts were too jumbled for worship.

"See you this afternoon, then," Sara called as she went out the door.

"Have some hot tea," Ellie advised.

Mari watched them go and then tied an apron over her pretty new dress. She'd clear the breakfast dishes, set the table for the evening meal and then maybe she'd go lie down for a while. Give herself some time to think. She'd have most of the day to herself. It was rare to have time where nothing was required of her, and she could just relax.

But as the minutes passed, she began to feel more and more uneasy that she'd made the wrong decision. Why had she stayed home from church? Out of fear? Was she afraid that God wasn't calling her? Or was she afraid He was?

After a few minutes, the feeling that she belonged at church service with her newfound friends and family grew stronger.

She glanced at the clock, not sure what to do. She knew what she *wanted* to do. It would take more courage to go than to stay home. So she rallied her courage. Removing the work apron, she found her blue denim coat and helped herself to one of Sara's woolen scarves. Because services were at Roman Byler's chair shop, it was close enough to walk.

"I'm going!" she declared to the empty house. Chin firm, shoulders back, she marched out of the house.

The walk down the lane, across the road and down the road wasn't far. It was cold and windy, but Mari didn't mind because the sun was shining, and when she tipped her head just so, she could feel its warmth. And better yet, its promise of warmer days to come. Every step made her more determined. Church was where she belonged. It was where she wanted to be.

As she started up Roman and Fanny's short drive, the line of black buggies between the house and shop made her slightly queasy again. What if she was making a mistake? What if God wasn't really calling her? A terrible thought crossed her mind. What if she wasn't worthy? Could God really accept her after she'd doubted Him for so long?

She reached the barnyard and stood there, uncertain. No one was in sight. Everyone had gone into the big shop where Roman made his chairs. She could run back to Sara's and no one would be the wiser. She glanced around. The barnyard was still and quiet except for the sound of a loose piece of tin on the side of a small shed. Suddenly losing her nerve, she ducked into the open shed.

Bales of hay were stacked against the far wall, and something gray slinked out of the shadows. Mari saw that what she'd feared might be a rat was a fluffy tomcat.

The friendly creature trotted over and rubbed against Mari's ankle. She stooped to pet it, and then a wave of memories swept over her as the air was filled with sound.

From inside the house came the achingly poignant resonance of joined voices singing an Old German hymn. The song was more chanting than modern words put to music. At the beginning of each verse a single wavering voice began alone and then a chorus of interwoven voices joined in praise, rich and sweet and so beautiful that she found herself in tears. Not of sorrow or fear, but tears of pure joy.

Step by step, Mari was drawn from the shed into the yard. Trembling, weeping, she made her way to the door of the chair shop. She let herself into the warm reception area of the shop. Two young mothers were there, one nursing an infant, another changing a toddler on a wide window seat. Both women stopped to smile at her, but neither spoke, unwilling to risk disturbing the singers in the main room of the building.

Mari removed her coat and added it to a pile on a chair, then quietly entered the much larger room. Workbenches and power saws had been moved so that rows of benches could be arranged in the open area. According to tradition, men and older boys sat on one side, women, girls and small children on the other. All three rooms opened into one another and were filled with worshippers. Everyone, other than a few elders, was standing, still singing the first hymn. There were many stanzas, and some hymns lasted more than half an hour. They'd not yet begun *The Loblied*, which was always the second hymn of every service.

Susanna King, Hannah's daughter, was in the last row, closest to the back of the room, and when she saw Mari, her round little face broke into a wide smile. Susanna moved over to make room for Mari and then took up the hymn again, her croaking voice never quite meshing with the others but filled with joyous enthusiasm. Mari drew in a deep breath and joined in. Susanna offered to share her hymnal, but Mari shook her head. She knew every note and every word by heart.

As everyone finished the last verse and began to

settle onto the wooden benches, Mari glanced over to the men's side of the room. At the same instant, James, sitting in the fourth row, looked in her direction. Their gazes met and held. James smiled at her and nodded. Mari smiled back, felt a rush of heat in her cheeks and sank back onto her seat. A shiver of excitement ran through her, and her eyes misted with tears once more.

It felt right that she should be there. It felt safe and good, and she felt enveloped by the unity of the people around her. Suddenly she found herself wondering why she had struggled with the decision to come. She didn't feel like a fish out of water; she felt as though she had come home after being on a long journey.

The *vorsinger*, an older man with a long white beard and a cheerful round face, stood and began the second hymn. Behind Mari, a group of boys filed in, whispering among themselves. They found seats at the back of the men's section on the adjoining porch, and as everyone rose to join in the hymn, Mari saw her Zachary was among them.

Susanna reached over and touched her arm and smiled at her again. "Sing," she urged.

And Mari did just that, giving herself over to the familiar worship service, and setting aside her worries and her fears to let the peace of God's grace flow over her.

When the last hymn had been sung and the congregation broke for the midday meal, Mari remained where she was, her hands clasped. Eyes closed, she prayed silently, barely hearing the sounds of benches being moved, children running and laughing and women calling out directions to get the tables set for the meal. At last, when she had poured her heart out to God, she

sighed with relief and opened her eyes, feeling a bit as
if she'd been wrung through her grandmother's old-
fashioned wringer washing machine.

Slowly Mari rose, taking in the activity around her.
Although tables were already set up and young girls
were laying out the place settings, there was plenty left
to do. In the past few weeks she'd attended communal
meals often enough to know what needed to be done,
and she found it easy to join in. She was just leaning
over to pick up the bench she'd been sitting on when
James's sister, Mattie, caught her eye.

Mari smiled. She was used to seeing Mattie with at
least one baby on her hip, but neither Timothy nor William was anywhere to be seen. Their father might have
them, but it was more likely that one of the other women
had swept the twins away, giving Mattie a much-needed
break.

"Good Sabbath," Mattie greeted her.

Mari smiled. "Good Sabbath," she repeated, setting
the bench down when she realized that Mattie was
headed her way to speak to her. "Where are the babies?"

"I have no idea. Someone has them, I suppose." She
chuckled, and Mari chuckled with her.

"I didn't see you when service started this morning,"
Mattie said, the bench between them. She was wearing
a plain black Sunday dress.

Mari smoothed the scarf that covered most of her
hair. Mattie was always pleasant to her, but Mari could
always feel an underlying current of tension between
them. James had warned Mari that Mattie was concerned about their friendship, but Mari kept hoping
that with time, his sister would realize that she had no
intention of kidnapping him and carrying him out into

the big bad world. Didn't Mattie realize that world was what Mari had been running from when she came to Seven Poplars?

"I…I wasn't feeling well this morning," Mari explained. "But then…I felt better." She watched Susanna King carry a big bowl of macaroni salad toward the buffet table.

"Well, it's good to have you here with us." Mattie smoothed the bodice of her dress. "I understand you're seeing the bishop regularly and beginning classes to prepare for baptism."

"I am." Mari nodded, still feeling a little emotional from the service. "I hope to be baptized next year."

"And become a full member of the community?" Mattie asked.

Only then did Mari pick up on a certain tone to Mattie's voice. Mattie didn't seem pleased. "That's my intention," she said, taking a quick glance around, hoping James was nearby. Usually, Mari didn't talk with Mattie without James.

"Well, I'm very happy for you and for your son. I hope that you find peace here." Mattie hesitated. "But it's also my hope…" She exhaled and then started again. "Mari, I'm just going to come out and say this."

Now Mari was really beginning to feel uncomfortable. She was in a big room with at least thirty people, and yet suddenly she felt alone. "Yes?"

"You know how much my little brother means to me. You know how close we are."

Mari nodded, thinking to herself that Mattie was speaking of him almost as if he were still the little boy she had raised after their mother passed away. But it didn't seem right to say that. She just stayed quiet and listened.

"I just… I think you need to be absolutely certain that your desire to be a part of our community isn't—" She glanced away as if trying to get control of her emotions. "Mari, what I'm trying to say is that I'm worried that you're joining church in the hopes that James will marry you."

Mari felt a sudden rush of tears. She was tempted to just walk away. She was hurt that Mattie would suggest such a thing, but then hadn't she wondered the same thing just a few hours earlier?

Mari took a breath and slowly turned her gaze to meet Mattie's. The suggestion stung, but she had to admire Mattie for being willing to come directly to her. "I can't…I can't say that I don't care for your brother because I do, but I want you to know, Mattie, that I'm joining the church because this is where I belong." Her voice caught in her throat. "God is calling me to come back to the Plain life I knew as a child, and I've realized since coming to Seven Poplars that this is where I was supposed to end up. It's our home now, my son's and mine." She took a breath, feeling steadier. "And as far as wanting to be baptized just so I can marry James, that wouldn't make sense because I was already approached with the opportunity to enter a possible match with James and I said no."

"James asked you to marry him?" Mattie asked, clearly shocked.

"No." Mari shook her head. "Someone approached Sara to make a possible match between James and me." She gave a little laugh that was without much humor.

"The person who hired Sara wanted to remain un-named. I actually wondered if it was you."

"But James didn't initiate it?"

She shook her head.

Mattie crossed her arms over her chest. "I see."

Mari leaned down and picked up the bench. "I should get this to a table. It looks like it's time for the first seating."

Mattie sighed. "Mari, it wasn't my intention to hurt you. I only—"

"It's all right, Mattie." Mari didn't look at her. "I understand. You're only looking out for James and I'm glad." Emotion filled her voice. "I'm glad you are, be-cause he deserves that. Now if you'll excuse me." Then she walked away.

Chapter Thirteen

After the morning services, James joined some other men outside and stood in the open carriage shed talking to Charley Byler. The sky looked as if it was going to rain. Church elders, married men and visitors were already seated in the chair shop, being served by the women. James usually waited until the second seating so that he could eat with his younger friends. Charley was telling him and the others about a new driving mare that he'd bought but James was only half listening.

Mari hadn't come to church with Sara and Ellie. Sara had explained that Mari hadn't been feeling well. James had been concerned and tempted to go check on her, but then had thought better of it. He could only imagine what Mattie would have to say. And Sara had assured him it was nothing for him to worry about. But then Mari had appeared, just as service began. Had she really just been feeling poorly, then felt better and decided to come after all, or was she experiencing spiritual doubts? When James first returned, even though he knew it was right for him, it still wasn't easy.

"James?"

He looked to see Mattie standing apart from the group of men. "Could I speak to you?"

She had one of the twins in her arms. Presumably, one of the other women had the other infant and the two older boys. That was the thing about community. A mother of young children could always count on help at any gathering. Relatives, friends and neighbors were always prepared to care for hungry, tired or rambunctious kids.

"Mattie looks like someone plucked the feathers off her favorite setting hen," Charley said, elbowing James playfully in the side.

James chuckled as he walked to meet her. But Charley was right. He could see by her strained face that she was upset. He wondered if one of the boys had misbehaved. "Something wrong?" he asked.

She motioned toward their buggy on the far side of the yard. Drops of rain sprinkled across his face. "I need to talk to you. Privately."

He glanced around. There were men in the barn, teenagers near the back of the house, women walking between the house and the building that housed the chair shop and factory. "Too cold out here in the yard for the baby," James said, taking the infant from her. The child was bundled in blankets, but the wind had turned raw. "Wait," he said. "Over there." He led the way to a toolshed. Inside, it was sheltered against the weather. He closed the door behind them. "Now, what's so important that—"

"I've been talking to Mari Troyer," she interrupted. He could barely see her face in the shadowy shed, but her posture was stiff, and he could almost feel the heat of her anger. "She said that someone approached Sara about a match for her. With you. When were you going to tell me? After the banns were read?"

He looked at her in disbelief and shook his head. "I have no idea what you're talking about."

"You know how I feel about this. I like Mari, but she's not right for you. Marriage is all about families. And if you marry her, you could tear our family apart." She gazed up at him, her eyes teary. "Are you willing to risk that?"

James was caught between feeling bad that Mattie was so upset and a strange excitement. Someone thought he and Mari should court? Who? Who would go to the matchmaker without telling him? It didn't make sense. Mari wasn't even a member of the church yet. Anyone who knew him well enough to know he secretly carried feelings for Mari would know he would never marry outside the church. He gazed down at his sister. "You're telling me that *Mari* told you that? You must have misunderstood."

"*Ne*, she told me not ten minutes ago. There's no misunderstanding. Didn't I warn you about this? I knew you were becoming too involved with her and her son. Was it you, James? Did you ask Sara to arrange a marriage?"

Still stunned, he stared back at her. "It's news to me," he said. "Who would be making a match for me?"

"I suppose she could have been telling an untruth, but she seemed sincere. She said that she'd refused the match. I don't know what to think. Why would she say such a thing, if it isn't true?"

Mari refused? His heart sank. "I can't say it any plainer, Mattie. I haven't proposed marriage to anyone. And I certainly didn't go to Sara."

The baby started to whimper, and he passed him back to Mattie.

"So, you didn't ask Sara to arrange a match between you and Mari?"

"No, I didn't."

She hesitated. "I saw you watching her during service."

He didn't reply. He just stood there.

"I thought... I'm sorry, brother. I was hurt by the thought that you might ask—"

"I just told you. I didn't."

Mattie sighed. "I'm sorry." She reached out with one hand and squeezed his arm. "I know you think I'm an interfering busybody. But you mean so much to me, to my children. I couldn't bear to see you make such a mistake."

He gazed out into the barnyard. He didn't know why he was upset. Mari had told him they were just friends. Anything he had read into their relationship was just his own wishful thinking. "I need to straighten this out," he told his sister.

"*Ya*, go to Sara. If Mari wasn't honest with me, you should know it."

"No, Sara's not who I need to talk to."

James found Mari in the reception area of the chair shop. She and Rebecca were carrying large pitchers of apple cider to the main showroom where the midday meal was being served. He stepped in front of her. "I have to talk to you."

"In a few minutes?" Mari asked, her mind seeming elsewhere. "Right now I have to—"

"Now," James insisted. He took the pitcher from her

and set it down on a table that held wood-stain color charts. "Please."

"I'll come back for it," Rebecca told Mari. She took one look at James and hurried off.

James took Mari's hand. "Come with me." Before she could protest, he led her through an office door and closed it behind them.

The room held a desk, a filing cabinet and several chairs. The outside wall was now taken up with a large window that opened on the yard. Although he didn't turn on a light, they could clearly see people walking past the window. The thought passed his mind that they could also see him and Mari. He didn't care.

"What is it?" Mari asked. "Has—"

Again, he cut her off. "Mattie said that you told her that someone asked Sara to arrange a match between you and me. Is that true?"

Mari stared up at him, wishing the floor would open up and swallow her. She wanted to look away, but she didn't.

"Is it true?" he repeated.

She couldn't tell if he was angry or hurt, but he was clearly upset. "Yes. Sara came to me and said so. She wouldn't say who had asked her."

"But you refused?"

Her mouth went dry. She could only nod.

"Why, Mari?" When she didn't answer, he continued, "Is it because you're not staying here? Because you want to take Zachary and go back to the English?"

"No." She shook her head again. "That's not what I want," she whispered. "I wasn't sure before, but I'm sure now. I belong here."

He took hold of her shoulders. His touch was gentle

but firm. She sensed that if she pulled away, he wouldn't stop her, but she couldn't take a step. She could feel that there was something real between them, almost as solid as if she could see and taste it.

"I need you to be honest with me. Did you say no because you think of me as only a friend?" he demanded, his eyes searching her. "That you…" He stopped and started again. "That you don't see me any other way? That you could never see me as anything more than a friend?"

Mari didn't know what to say. If she told him she saw him as only a friend, it would be over. She wouldn't have to hear him tell her she'd been right in her decision. But there was something about the way he was looking at her that made her think something more was going on between them. The barest hint of possibility made her brave. "No," she whispered. "That isn't why I said no. But *you* said we were just friends. You said it over and over again."

"Because *you* said we were just friends. I knew within days, hours, maybe minutes of meeting you that my feelings for you were more."

Mari held her breath. They were practically in a fishbowl; anyone outside could see them standing so close, gazing into each other's eyes, but she couldn't move away from him. "I don't know what I want," she managed.

"I know what I want. I want you to stay in Seven Poplars," he said quietly. "I want you to be baptized into our faith, and I want us to walk out together. And if this is what I think it is, what I feel in my heart, I want you to be my wife."

She began to tremble. Tears clouded her eyes. "You

want to marry me?" she murmured huskily. "You want to be Zachary's father?"

"With all my heart," he assured her. "I want to be your husband and Zachary's father. But do you feel the same? You have to be absolutely honest here. Don't worry about hurting my feelings." He took a deep breath. "Are you willing to give us a chance to find out if we're meant to be together…as a family?"

"Yes," she answered. "Yes, I think I…" She looked down and then back up at him again. "If I could do anything, it would be marry you, love you."

He took both of her hands in his.

"But…I need time," Mari went on. "And *that's* what I told Sara. It wasn't that I didn't…" The words stuck in her throat. "It isn't you I'm not sure of. It's me. I have to know that I'm coming back to the church because it's what God wants me to do, not just because…because I think I love you." Suddenly, she became aware of a face close to the outside of the window. "James, someone's—"

"It's Martha." He looked from the window back to Mari again. "And I think we should give her something to see." James pulled Mari against him, tipped her chin with gentle fingers and kissed her full on the mouth.

Chapter Fourteen

"Why are you smiling?" James asked, tilting his menu so he could see her over the top.

Mari lowered her menu. "Why are *you* smiling?" she teased, leaning over so he could hear her above the hubbub of a birthday party going on on the far side of the restaurant.

They were sitting across from each other at a table for two in a pizza place near Byler's store. They'd made plans days earlier for him to pick her up from work and stop for supper. While they spent most of their time together in the presence of others at church, or on visiting Sunday or at a friend's or family member's house, they had both agreed that they would spend time together alone once a week. Now that they were officially courting, it was important to them that they spend time really getting to know each other. Secretly, they called it *date night*. It was an Englisher term the Amish never used, and Martha certainly would have disapproved, but it was a little joke Mari and James shared.

"*I'm* smiling because I've looked forward to this all

week and now finally here you are." He slid his hand across the table toward hers.

It was all Mari could do to make herself pull her hand away before they touched. She and James had discussed their idea of spending time alone together with both Sara and Preacher Caleb, and everyone had agreed that because of their age, it would be okay to occasionally go somewhere alone. But they had also agreed that the rules of propriety had to be followed. Among the Amish, there was no kissing until marriage, and there wasn't supposed to be hand-holding, at least not until a wedding date was set, but since they had already broken the kissing rule in front of their entire church, they'd both agreed to take care in their physical expression of their feelings for each other.

But now that they were courting, she wanted to hold hands with him. And she wanted to hurry up and marry him just so he could kiss her again.

James sighed, frowned and glanced at his menu. "I'm so glad you like pizza. It's one thing I haven't been able to give up since I came back."

"I don't think being Amish means we can't eat pizza." She picked up her menu. She didn't know why she was looking. They'd end up getting the same thing they always got: a large veggie pizza with red peppers, artichokes, mushrooms and eggplant.

"It doesn't, but there are some people who think being in a place like this—" he lowered his voice "—where alcohol is served, is wrong."

She nodded, setting aside her menu. She was so happy to see James; they didn't get a chance to see each other every day. On days when she didn't see him, it seemed as if she constantly wanted to tell him something. There were definitely times when she wished they had phones to call each other, but as Sara had pointed out to her, in some ways it made being together better. Maybe there was something to be said about absence making the heart grow fonder.

A waiter came by and took their order; sure enough, they agreed on their usual. Once he was gone, Mari leaned back in her chair. She'd dressed with extra care, wearing another new dress Sara had made her; this one was rose colored. And with it, she wore a matching scarf over her hair. "Did you ever drink alcohol when you were living among the English?" she asked him.

"I tried it." He shrugged. "I had a beer a couple of times. I even tried a shot of whiskey once." He shuddered. "If that's what makes a man a man, I guess I'm not." He slid his hand across the table again and just touched her fingertips. "You?"

"I tried one of Ivan's beers once." She made a face. "That was the worst stuff I've ever tasted in my life. I spit it out in the sink."

He laughed with her.

"I've never understood why Ivan and his friends liked to drink alcohol," she went on. "I don't understand why they liked the way it made them act." She looked down at their hands on the table, almost touching, yet not quite. "Ivan wasn't a very nice person when he drank beer."

When James didn't say anything, she looked up at him. "I'm sorry. Does it bother you when I talk about Ivan?"

"Not the fact that you were married to him," he explained. "Just that he didn't treat you the way you deserved to be treated. That's what I find upsetting."

Mari could feel her heart swelling. James was so sweet. So kind and good to her. She could barely believe that all of this was happening. She was going to join the church and be baptized. And in a year or two, she and James were going to be married. She knew that the idea of courting was to get to know each other, but they'd agreed within days of their kiss in the chairshop office, it was just a formality. They were getting married. There was no doubt in either of their minds.

"I try not to think about Ivan as being a big mistake, because I never felt that Zachary was a mistake. I mean…I wish we'd been married first. Before…" She met his gaze. One of the best things about James was that he was so nonjudgmental, particularly about her past. He told her all the time that what she was doing *today*, what she planned to do *tomorrow* with her life, was what mattered. She felt a faint blush. "You know what I mean. I regret Ivan, but I don't regret Zachary."

"Two root beers," the young waiter announced, setting mugs on the table between them. He pulled straws out of his apron and placed them on the table. "And your pizza's in the oven. Be right out."

"Thanks," James and Mari said in unison. They both laughed as they opened their straws, dropped them into their glasses and took a sip. They were always talking over each other, saying the same thing.

"Okay, so I have to admit, I'm still curious as to who went to Sara to arrange our match," James said.

"Me, too," Mari agreed. "But Sara won't say a word. She said it was an agreement between her and the other party, and it was their wish that we not know."

He played with the paper from his straw. "I just can't imagine who it could have been."

"Well, we know it wasn't your sister," she said with a grimace.

He laughed. "No, it wasn't Mattie, but she's coming around. I think she's beginning to see that we really are meant to be together."

"She's been very nice to me. Never a harsh or critical word. I think she genuinely believes that she was looking out for your best interests when she said she didn't think we should court."

"She still feels guilty about that. I think that job she got me was her way of trying to make up for it."

"Oh, the new job! I'm sorry. You met with clients yesterday. I completely forgot." His sister had an English woman who bought eggs from them regularly and when the customer had said she was looking for a contractor to build her new house, Mattie had introduced her to James. "How did it go?"

"Great. I'm hired. We go to contract next week. I'm building a three-bedroom house with a garage. She may want a barn, as well."

Mari clapped. "That's wonderful news. I'm so happy for you."

"I'm happy for *us*." He beamed. "I'll be able to save plenty of money. I was thinking that after we marry we'd take a trip. A honeymoon."

She stared at him. "Do Amish do that?"

"Sure. Sometimes. Well, mostly we go visit out-of-state relatives, but I was thinking maybe we could go to the beach. You said you've always wanted to swim in the ocean."

She looked down at her Amish-style dress. "I'm pretty sure the bishop wouldn't go for me in a bathing suit."

"So we'll just wade in. Together."

"Sounds wonderful," she said, unable to take her eyes from his.

He took her hand in his before she could pull away and squeezed it before letting go. "I think every day we spend together is going to be wonderful, Mari Troyer."

"Catch!" James, who'd been washing dishes, tossed a bowl to Mari.

"Don't!" she warned, but the brown pottery bowl was already in the air. She made a grab for it and managed to snatch it out of the air. "Don't do that," she protested. "What if I'd missed?"

He laughed. "But you didn't, did you? You have a good eye and good instincts. You need to trust yourself more."

"Who says I don't?"

His beautiful eyes gleamed. "We have to risk to get the most out of life."

"I'd say I'm risking a lot walking out with you," she teased.

He grinned at her, and her heart skipped a beat. Funny, sweet and tender, James was everything she'd ever wanted in a man. She couldn't believe that they were officially courting. He'd made both her and her son so happy that it was like a dream come true.

James rinsed a serrated bread knife under the faucet, shook off the dripping water and raised one brow in a mischievous expression.

"Don't you dare."

He shrugged, offered a sad face and meekly passed the knife to her, handle first.

She suppressed a giggle, dried the knife and returned

it to the wooden rack. "Sara won't let you in her hospitality kitchen if you keep taking chances with her good dishes," she admonished. It was a Monday evening and the two of them had volunteered to help Charley and Miriam chaperone an impromptu meeting of the Gleaners in Sara's barn. The youth group had met to make plans to help out elderly or infirm members of the Amish community on Saturdays. It was after 9:00 p.m. The boys and girls had already departed, and the four adults were just finishing the cleanup.

"Seriously, Mari," James said. "You would make a good catcher. I think you should try out for the women's softball team this spring."

"Here in Seven Poplars? An Amish team?" He nodded, and she asked, "Are they all unmarried girls who play?"

"No. Lots of young mothers. Miriam coaches. Rebecca, Grace, even Addy plays. And Miriam—"

"What about Miriam?" She came into the kitchen with a tray of glasses. Like all Hannah's daughters, Mari thought she was a beautiful young woman who appeared younger than her years. Miriam wore a neat plum-colored dress with a white apron and a crisp white prayer *kapp*. And, being Miriam, there was a bounce in her step. It was difficult to remember that she was old enough to be the mother of two children and not a Gleaner herself. "This is the last of it," Miriam pronounced. "Charley's sweeping up."

James took the tray. "I was just telling her about your softball team."

Miriam chuckled. "We're always looking for players. No tryouts. If you want to play, show up in sneakers. But I warn you, James throws a mean pitch. When we challenge the men's team, we make them hit opposite-handed." She beamed with good humor. "We'd love to have you join us, Mari."

"Mari!" Charley pushed open the door from the main room. "Bishop Atlee is here to see you. You, too, James."

"The bishop?" James looked at Mari. "Do you have any idea what this is about?"

She shook her head. She undid her apron, hung it on a hook and hurried to meet Bishop Atlee. He was the one who'd been giving her instructions on joining the church, and she was scheduled to meet him again the following night. She couldn't imagine why he'd come to speak to her tonight.

As she approached the gray-haired man, Mari saw that his mood was somber. Behind her, Charley and Miriam called out a hasty good-night.

James glanced from the bishop to Mari. "Should I—" He hooked his thumb over his shoulder, indicating he could excuse himself.

"Ne." Bishop Atlee motioned to a table. "This concerns you both. I stopped at your house and Mattie told me that I'd find you here." He took a seat at the head of the table, and she and James sat to one side, facing him.

"This is awkward," the bishop said. "It's not a situation I've encountered before, and I've served in Seven Poplars for years." He was quiet for a moment, seeming to gather his thoughts. But the silence went on long enough for Mari to begin to feel uncomfortable.

"Mari," the bishop said, "it's my custom to always contact the previous church elders to inquire about the history of someone who wishes to become a member of our district. Soon after you began consulting with me,

I wrote to your old community. I wasn't prying. I simply had to confirm that you left your own church and entered the English world before accepting baptism."

"Yes." Mari nodded. "I can see how that would be something you'd need to know." Though her running away had caused much scandal at the time, she'd been unbaptized. The difference was a difficult one for outsiders to understand. Accepting baptism into the Amish church and then leaving was a terrible sin. It meant that the person had broken their faith, not only with the community but with God. That person would be formally shunned. Members could not eat with them. They could not ride in a car or a buggy driven by the shunned person and, in most cases, would not even speak to them.

Her aunt and uncle had refused to allow her to enter their home, but everyone in the county didn't accept their strict interpretation. Many, especially Sara, felt that Mari's family had been unnecessarily cruel, and their beliefs and actions had not prevented her from being welcomed into the Seven Poplars Amish neighborhood.

"This afternoon, I received this letter." He handed it to Mari. "You may read it." And to James, he said, "I'm afraid that plans for Mari's baptism and your marriage must be called off. She can't marry you because the current bishop states that she was already baptized into the Amish faith. Apparently, Mari made her promise to God and later went back on her word. Then she further compounded her error by coming to Seven Poplars and Sara's home under false pretenses." He folded his hands and placed them on the surface of the table. "I can't offer you membership into our church community at this time. I'm not saying it's not possible, ever. We can sit down and talk once we've both had time to think, but I know you understand that this changes everything."

Mari looked at Bishop Atlee and then back at the letter. Her hands shook so hard that she could barely make out the words. But the name at the bottom of the page was plain. The signature in tiny cramped letters was her uncle's. "My uncle wrote this?" she managed.

"Ya." Bishop Atlee folded his hands. "He recently became the bishop of his church. As your senior relative and your religious leader, he felt that he had to share this information with us."

She shook her head. "No. He couldn't have. That's not possible." She looked down at the letter again, hoping that she'd read it wrong.

"Mari, James…I'm so sorry," Bishop Atlee said, getting to his feet. "If you wish to discuss my decision further, I'll be at home on Saturday afternoon."

"There has to be some mistake," James protested.

"There has been," the bishop agreed. "And I'm afraid it was Mari who made it. But God is merciful. No one is beyond redemption. And if she truly repents of her rash actions, she can, in time, be forgiven." He nodded to them both and then walked out of the barn.

James stared at Mari. She could see the heartbreak on his face. "Is it true?" he asked. "Were you baptized?"

She tried to answer, but the words wouldn't come. How could he believe such a thing of her?

"I'm asking you, Mari. Say something."

"You actually think I'd lie to Sara…to you…to everyone about whether or not I was baptized?" She pushed her hands against the table and rose to her feet. "If you think that, you don't know me well enough to court me. And if you think that—" she choked on her tears "—you'll never know me well enough to marry me."

"Mari—"

Ignoring him, she ran to the door. He started after her, but she whirled on him, her face streaked with tears. "I'd believe you," she cried. "No matter what you told me, I'd believe you."

"Mari, please—"

"No, James. It's over between us."

"We have to talk about this."

"There's nothing more to say. I did make mistakes when I was nineteen, and I made another one when I thought we could have a future together. Goodbye, James." She ran through the darkness toward Sara's house.

Chapter Fifteen

James ran after Mari to the house, catching up to her at the porch. He asked her again if they could talk, but she refused. She went inside, closing the door behind her.

For a moment he just stood there, stunned. He didn't know what to do. If he and Mari couldn't discuss the problem, how could they work it out? He wanted to believe her, but the facts seemed to state otherwise. He wanted to put his arms around her and tell her that he would make everything right—that they would be married as they planned. But he couldn't let himself be blinded by love. If there was a chance that she had deceived him, it would be difficult to get past it. But to his shame, he had to admit that it wasn't breaking the *ordnung* that mattered to him as much as whether or not she'd told him an untruth.

James's sister's warnings rose in his mind as he walked to the barn. Could Mattie be right about Mari breaking his heart? In his gut, he knew that Mari wasn't capable of such a ruse. There *had* to be an explanation. But what was it? One of them had to be wrong. Was it Mari, or was it the bishop?

The questions preyed on James's mind all the way home. He wasn't ready to give up on Mari and Zachary, but her refusal to talk to him was disturbing. When he put his horse in the barn and went into the house, it was dark. Everyone was asleep. He lit a single propane lamp, took a Bible from a shelf in the living room and sat down at the kitchen table to read.

The familiar words that usually brought him so much peace didn't answer his questions. He closed the Bible, bowed his head and prayed.

Mattie found him there sometime after midnight. "Brother, you're up late," she said as she padded into the kitchen in her fuzzy slippers. Her hair was down around her shoulders, and she was wearing a robe over her long nightdress. "Is something wrong?"

He sighed.

She took a seat across from him. "Whatever it is, you can tell me." She waited, then asked, "Is it to do with Mari?"

He nodded. And when she said nothing, he found himself telling her the whole tale. She didn't say a word until he finished.

"And Mari insists that she told the truth?" Mattie asked quietly. He nodded. "And you believe her?" He nodded again. She took his hand and squeezed it.

"Mattie, I know you're against this marriage but…" He could feel his eyes tearing up, and he was embarrassed. "I love her."

"James, you're mistaken. I'm *not* against Mari. I'm against anything that would take you away from me, from our family and from our church." There was no accusation in her voice. This was his Mattie, the person he'd confided in and depended on since he was a child.

"I told you that I would never leave the faith again. If Mari and I marry, we'll make our home here, our faith will be hers."

"And she makes you happy?"

"She does."

"I've watched Mari, and despite my concerns, I do believe she loves you. All I want, all I've ever wanted, is your happiness. And if it's Mari who makes you happy, then I'll accept and love her, too."

"But this…" He shook his head. "I don't know what to make of it. Why would her own uncle tell an untruth?"

"Sara believes her to be unbaptized, doesn't she?"

He nodded. "Yes, but they never went to the same church and this… It would have been a long time ago." Then he let the question that had troubled him most fall between them. "And if Mari is telling the truth, why did she shut me out? Why was she so angry?" He rested his forehead on one hand. "It makes no sense to me. All I said was 'Is it true?' What kind of man wouldn't ask that question?"

"Maybe asking it caused her to doubt you," Mattie suggested. Her oval face was soft in the lamplight. "And maybe she was so hurt that she just lashed out like our sweet colt did last summer when he caught his leg in that wire. He was in so much pain that he couldn't think straight."

He raised his gaze to hers. "What should I do, Mattie? What would you do?"

"It's different. I'm a woman. I know what I'd do, but what's important is what *you* want to do."

"I don't know." He shrugged. "My first impulse is to hire a driver. Go straight to Wisconsin. Find out the truth for myself. Clear Mari's name."

She laid her palm on the kitchen table. "Then that's what you should do. Go first thing in the morning."

"You don't think I'm a fool for doing that?"

She chuckled. "I think you're a fool if you don't."

Mari took another towel from the laundry basket and pinned it on the clothesline. Sheets flapped in the wind as the late-morning sun warmed the air. She loved the smell of freshly washed clothes that had been line-dried, and normally she didn't mind doing the wash. Today, her heart wasn't in the familiar chore.

Although it was Saturday morning, a refrigeration problem the previous night had forced the butcher shop to close. She would rather have been at work. Gideon had assured everyone that they would receive their regular pay for the missed hours, but she regretted the forced holiday. When she was working, it was easier to forget that her uncle's letter had ruined everything between her and James, and that she had only compounded the problem by refusing to discuss the problem with him.

Her first thought had been that James's failure to believe her meant that he didn't love her enough, that he didn't trust her. Her own pride and insecurity had caused an ugly exchange of words—words she hadn't meant and would give anything to take back.

Thinking about it rationally, James hadn't accused her of lying to him, he'd simply asked if her uncle's accusation was true. She couldn't blame him for that. All she would have had to do was deny it. Her behavior was both immature and hurtful to the man she loved. And now she would pay the price. And she couldn't blame Bishop Atlee. He was acting as the shepherd of his church. He'd not accused her or rejected her. He'd simply told her that her baptism and wedding would be postponed.

Sara, as always, remained her rock. When she'd spilled out her story to Sara, her friend had sympathized with her and had offered her usual dose of sage advice. "Baptisms aren't performed in secret," she exclaimed. "Not even in the wilds of Wisconsin. I'd have heard if you'd been baptized."

Of course, Sara was right. When a young man or woman pledged his or her life to the faith, the entire community stood witness. Her uncle's false tale couldn't hold water, because other members of the church would verify her story. She didn't know why he had done it. She wouldn't want to think that he held such animosity against her that he would want to ruin her opportunity to return to the Amish faith and to make a good marriage.

Sara had only shrugged. She would write her own letters, she insisted. She had many contacts in Wisconsin, and she would ask them to confirm Mari's innocence. "It might take time," Sara said, "but we'll straighten this mess out and get you and James back together."

Mari wasn't so sure. Five days had now passed without a word from James. She hadn't seen him and he hadn't sent word by way of anyone else. It was obvious the life she had dreamed of these past few weeks was over before it ever began. Of course she realized that staying in Seven Poplars didn't depend on her marrying James or anyone else. Her precious son was happy here, and she was, too. But she'd wanted more. She'd dreamed of being James's wife, of having children together. Because of her own foolish words, that dream had dissolved. Now he might never allow her to mend the breech between them. And that loss would linger with her the rest of her days.

She reached for another towel, but her basket wasn't where she thought she'd left it. Puzzled, she looked around, then ducked under the line of wash.

And there stood James, wooden clothespins in his mouth and a damp sheet in his hands. He appeared to be looking for the corner of the sheet, but he'd succeeded only in making a muddle of it.

She laughed. She'd never been so happy to see anyone in her life.

He laughed, and the pins dropped out of his mouth onto the grass. Then he gave her a smile that melted her heart.

"Oh, James." She tried to find words, but they wouldn't come. What did come were tears.

He dropped the sheet and took hold of her shoulders. He pulled her close and looked down into her eyes. "It's all right," he said. "Stop crying. I can't stand it when you cry."

She cried harder, and he cradled her head against his chest. "I thought you were never going to speak to me again," she managed between gasps and sobs. "I was so wrong to run away from you like that, to say such things. I didn't mean it, James. I didn't. I love you so much...and now—"

"Now it's all right, Mari. Everything's all right. I went to Wisconsin and brought back proof that you were telling the truth."

"You went to Wisconsin?" She sniffed. "How?"

"Stop crying and I'll tell you." He pulled a handkerchief from his pocket and wiped away her tears.

"Why did my uncle tell such lies about me?"

"He's ill. My guess is that he's probably suffering from Alzheimer's. Your aunt says he's not himself. She says it comes and goes. Some days he gets lost on his own farm and one of his grandchildren has to find him and bring him back."

"But he said he was the bishop."

"And he is. No one in the church will take that office from him, but his preachers are understanding. They help him perform his duties. But a neighbor said the mental loss has done nothing good for his temperament. He did you a great wrong, but he needs our prayers more than condemnation." James took both her hands in his. "Can you do that? Can you have the grace to forgive him? Not just for this, but for all the ways he failed you? He should never have turned his back on you the way he did. To turn you away when you came to him in need. It's not what we're taught."

She pressed her lips together. "I'm sorry you had to hear those things."

"I'm not. But what's in the past is in the past. Whatever he's done, it's not for us to judge him. He will have to face a higher judgment." James took hold of her chin and raised it tenderly. "Can you pray for him?"

She nodded. Whatever bitterness she'd felt had evaporated with the sight of James's face. He was right. Who was she to judge anyone? "Can you forgive me?" she asked him.

"There's nothing to forgive. You were hurting and you reacted." He took her hand. "I want you to come to Bishop Atlee with me. We'll tell him the good news."

Doubt pierced her joy. "Will he believe you? Did you bring letters from anyone else?"

"No letters but something better." He grinned again. "Caleb. When Mattie told Rebecca that I was going to Wisconsin, she insisted that her husband accompany me. Caleb is one of our preachers. Everyone knows his word is good, and he witnessed the same statements that I did. He spoke with your uncle. We both did. And we could see that he wasn't behaving rationally."

"And Caleb will speak for me?"

"He will. He was going home to see Rebecca and the children, and then he's going straight to the bishop."

"We have to tell Sara," Mari said. "She believed me, but we have to share this wonderful news with her."

He looked down at the sheet on the ground. "Maybe we'd best finish this chore first. I don't want to be the one who tells Sara that I kept you from hanging out her laundry."

Mari looked at the wet sheet and then at him. "And what do we do about this?"

"Hang it up and hope for the best," he ventured.

"You seem to be all thumbs when it comes to hanging wash," she teased.

He chuckled. "That's what Mattie says."

She found a corner of the sheet and passed it to him. "So your sister knows you went to Wisconsin?"

"She knows," he replied as he retrieved the fallen clothespins. "She's the one who urged me to go."

"Then she won't stand in the way of our courting?"

"No, darling, Mattie won't stand in our way. It eases my heart that the two women I love best aren't at odds, but what Mattie wanted would never have made a difference. As much as I care for her, it was never her decision." He leaned over the clothesline until they were nose to nose and he gazed into her eyes. "You're the one I intend to marry, if you'll have me."

"I will," she promised. "I will, forever and ever."

Epilogue

Mari paused by her kitchen sink to gaze out the open window. It was a beautiful spring day, warm and full of the sweet scents of herbs and the fresh-turned earth of her kitchen garden. Just outside, a Carolina wren whistled a merry tune as it scratched at the base of the bird feeder James and Zachary had built for her the previous fall.

In the meadow, Mari could see Zachary and James heading toward the house, leading a brown-and-white pony hitched to a child's cart. She needed to get supper on the table; she was running behind because she'd been cooking for the following day's worship service. But now that Mari had everything ready for the Sabbath, she could take the time to feed her own family properly.

Tomorrow would be their second wedding anniversary, but because it was also a church Sunday, she thought it would be fine with James if they celebrated a day early. It didn't seem possible that so much time had passed since they'd stood in front of the elders and pledged their lives to each other. It seemed like only yesterday. *I'm happy*, she thought, *happier than I ever would have thought possible*. Life with James fulfilled all her dreams, for her and for Zachary.

The change in her son since they'd come to Seven Poplars was more than she'd hoped for. All he'd needed was a place to belong. And a father to guide him. Now, at eleven, going on twelve, he had not only grown in height and breadth, but in maturity and wisdom. He went willingly to school and kept up a B average, but his first love was being in the woodshop with James. Zachary said that he wanted to be a carpenter, and Mari thought that was a fine ambition. After all, hadn't Lord Jesus been a carpenter?

The odor of browning biscuits drew her away from the window and her musing, and she grabbed a hot mitt and opened the oven door.

"Something smells good," James said.

Mari smiled as a warm joy filled her. Would the day ever come that she could see him and not feel a burst of happiness? She hoped not.

"Zach will be in in a minute—he's putting his pony up." James came up behind her, slipped an arm around her waist and gently kissed the nape of her neck.

"Behave yourself," she protested, laughing. "What if Zachary comes in and sees you?"

James chuckled. "And what if he does?"

Laughing, she pushed him away and went to the refrigerator for butter.

"I brought you something," he said.

Pleased, she turned to see him holding a brimming handful of wildflowers. "Oh."

"Happy anniversary," he said.

She blinked back tears and smiled at him. "Beautiful," she managed. Multicolored blooms cascaded out of the bouquet, prettier than anything a florist could have arranged. "Thank you."

"Thank you," he murmured, pulling her against him and kissing her mouth tenderly. "These last two years have been the best of my—" An indignant wail broke through his words, and he released her to turn toward the cradle. "And what's wrong with you?" he crooned. "Is *Dat*'s little man hungry?"

"I'll get him," Mari said.

"Let me." James crossed to the cradle and scooped up their six-week-old Samuel. "I haven't gotten to hold him all day. Isn't that so?" he murmured to the baby. He settled into the rocking chair, shifted Samuel onto his shoulder and began patting the infant's back.

Samuel let out a loud burp, and both Mari and James laughed. "So that's all he needed," Mari said.

"No, all he needed was some *Daddi* time," James teased.

"Supper ready?" Zachary asked as he came in the door. "I'm really hungry."

"Wash up and pour iced tea for you and your father," Mari said.

A few minutes later, Mari lowered her head and closed her eyes for grace. *Thank You for Your many blessings, for this food, for the roof over our heads and for our two healthy sons. Thank You for my good and loving husband,* she prayed silently. *And thank You Lord for making a place for me at Your table.*

Mari had no illusions that her future would be free from worries and loss, but with love and faith she also knew in her heart that as a family, they would find a way to make it through. They would strive to serve their community and their faith. And they would be happy forever and ever. Together. Because she was finally home…

* * * * *

Dear Reader,

I'm so pleased you're joining me again for another story of love and faith in the Amish community of Seven Poplars! The matchmaker, Sara Yoder, has certainly stirred things up, hasn't she? I don't know about you, but I love this character. Sara has the wisdom of our old friend from my previous books, Hannah Yoder, but there's something sassy about Sara I find appealing. She's someone I would love to be friends with.

In this story, you'll be meeting Mari Yoder, a young woman who left her Amish life in Wisconsin years ago, but, through circumstances, finds herself and her son in Sara's care. Mari isn't looking for a husband, and she certainly has no intentions of becoming Amish again. But there's something about Seven Poplars and the Amish community that makes her feel as if she's finally come home.

And then there's James Hostetler, the nicest guy you would ever want to meet, who befriends Mari, making no judgments on her past. They really are just friends. Or are they more? You'll just have to read on to find out!

Wishing you peace and joy,
Emma Miller